There goes the bride...

Darby sighed. Now that the moment had come for her to rendezvous with her husband-to-be, she couldn't quite summon the enthusiasm that she knew she should feel. But she was determined to give baby Sissy a family, and Chauncey had admitted that he was the baby's father. A marriage of convenience was the only way she'd be able to keep her best friend's baby...

Chauncey's aunt Patty sniffled, juggling the baby into the crook of her arm. "I'm so happy," she said, between hiccuping sighs. "After Chauncey's bout with mumps left him sterile all those years ago, I never thought he'd marry. Yet, here you are, willing to overlook that detail. And, in the process, you've given me more than I could have ever hoped for—a little grandniece."

Just then the wedding march began, and Patty whirled away and rushed outdoors. Leaving Darby stunned. Frozen.

As she waited for her cue, one word kept reverberating through her head.

Sterile...sterile...sterile...

Dear Reader,

Their ideal bedtime story starts with a deep voice
saying, "Hey, gorgeous," not "Once upon a time."
To them, "baby" is an endearment, not a stage of life!
Yep, Darby Simms is about to get a wake-up call.
She's about to become an "Accidental Mom"!

Lisa Bingham takes you on a tumultuous trip into
parenthood—as fashion designer Darby Simms takes
daredevil bachelor Christian Blake along for the ride
on a "daddy hunt" for her newly inherited baby girl!
Lisa Bingham is a well-known historical romance
author, now making a new name for herself with her
fourth contemporary romance novel.

Don't miss the companion novel to this—
Mary Anne Wilson's *Mismatched Mommy?*—
available right now.

Happy reading!

Debra Matteucci
Senior Editor and Editorial Coordinator
Harlequin Books
300 East 42nd Street
New York, NY 10017

Lisa Bingham

THE DADDY HUNT

Harlequin Books

TORONTO • NEW YORK • LONDON
AMSTERDAM • PARIS • SYDNEY • HAMBURG
STOCKHOLM • ATHENS • TOKYO • MILAN
MADRID • WARSAW • BUDAPEST • AUCKLAND

ISBN 0-373-16651-6

THE DADDY HUNT

Chapter One

Darby Simms exhaled, sending a puff of breath sky-ward and causing the tulle of her wedding veil to lift away from her eyes, then settle back into the same annoying position. There was no hope for the head-dress, absolutely none. No matter what Darby did, the hairpiece looked wilted and dingy, and when she moved, she swore that the faint odor of mothballs wafted into the air.

Grimacing, she supposed she shouldn't be so fas-tidious. She shouldn't wish for a beautiful gown of her own choosing and a veil made of yards and yards of lace as she had always imagined she would one day wear. There hadn't been time for such indulgences. Not when the nuptial ceremony had been arranged in less than a fortnight.

Lifting her skirts, she draped the scratchy net over one arm so that the cool, refrigerated air billowing from the vent caressed her skin. But the action didn't ease her restlessness as she'd hoped.

Automatically her eyes searched the pink and gilt-covered room, settling on a wardrobe next to an overstuffed settee. Curious, Darby opened one of the doors, then crowed in delight when she discovered an entertainment center, complete with a television set.

Why some interior decorator had decided to include a television in this room, Darby would never know. After all, weren't most brides caught up in the festivities to the exclusion of all else? Why would they want to be reminded of the outside world?

But even as the questions rolled into her head, Darby silently thanked that nameless decorator, whoever he or she might be. Right now, she needed a diversion. She'd been dressed and ready for more than an hour, but as her mother-in-law-to-be, Ida Fitch, kept reminding her with minute-by-minute updates, Darby's groom hadn't arrived yet. Darby punched the Power button in pique. At this moment, Chauncey's private jet was *still* circling the San Francisco International Airport waiting for ground clearance.

Darby sighed. If she'd known so much time would have elapsed before the ceremony would actually have begun, she would have remained in her jeans and T-shirt and ordered a pizza. As it was, she was trapped in a monstrosity of a dress, one made of layers of scratchy netting and a boned satin bustier.

Not for the first time, she cursed herself for agreeing to wear the horrible creation, but Ida had been so insistent, so adamant, so... overbearing, that Darby hadn't had the heart to say no.

"Heart," my aunt Fanny, a little voice inside her mocked. *You didn't have the nerve.*

Drawing her legs beneath her, Darby began to skip aimlessly through the channels. Her mood brightened ever so slightly when she saw the plethora of choices.

"Look, Sissy. They have cable," she remarked in an overly cheerful voice, peering down at the infant who lay on a pink-edged receiving blanket on the floor. Sissy—a.k.a. Sharece Nashton, heir to the Nashton china fortune, and Darby's ward—had also been dressed in tier upon tier of ruffles. Nevertheless, the baby appeared singularly unimpressed with her attire or the provided entertainment, and continued to chew on her fist. In fact, she looked positively bored.

"You could appear a little more enthused, you know," Darby stated teasingly, wagging the remote in Sissy's direction. "After all, I'm doing this for you, kid." Then she relented and added more seriously, "For you and me both. I couldn't leave you with strangers, now could I?"

Bending, Darby scooped the infant into her arms, absorbing the weight of her, the powder-fresh scent of her. Not for the first time, a tug in the region of her heart reminded Darby how dear this child had become to her. In the space of a few short weeks, she had grown to be the focus of Darby's life and Darby couldn't imagine being without the baby.

"We're a family, Sissy," she whispered in the infant's ear. "We'll make this work."

She was about to toss the channel selector onto the pillow, when Darby was caught by a picture flashing across the screen.

Her picture.

Hers and Sissy's.

"What in the world?" Automatically she juggled the baby and increased the volume as a woman with a sweep of blond hair and carefully applied makeup began to speak.

"*...And now the story of the week for The Gossip Exchange!*"

The screen faded into a grainy photograph, which could only have been retrieved from Darby's high school annual.

"*Nooo,*" Darby groaned, eyeing the awful hair and clothing, which had been all the rage ten years ago, but was the topic of good-natured ribbing in today's society.

"*Those who know her are calling Darby Simms the girl with the Midas touch.*"

The shot faded into a grade-school class photograph. Darby—eyes shut, hair scraped back in pigtails—sat holding the class identification placard.

"*She was born in Mayfield, Iowa, the only child of Maude and Henry Simms...*"

"Where did they get this stuff?" Darby whispered aloud. She certainly hadn't given the program any information—she'd never even heard of this show before.

But as the screen was filled with bootlegged copies of old home movies, Darby knew that the footage could only have been supplied by one source. Aunt Mavis. Darby's only living relative, she resided in a nursing home in Iowa, was all but blind, and hungry for company. Since Darby was only able to see her three or four times a year, she must have succumbed to the reporter's pressurings for information.

"*…. Upon the tragic death of her parents when she was thirteen, the community sponsored her in a contest for a special-needs scholarship to the exclusive Westwood Boarding School in Connecticut. It was there she met Eloise Nashton, heir to the Nashton china fortune.*"

Darby blinked when a photograph of Eloise— young, beautiful, poised—flashed into view.

"*The two became instant companions, enjoying a friendship that would endure until death cut it short.*"

There was a brief clip of a snowy hillside, the destructive path of an avalanche, and the flashing lights of a Swiss ambulance.

Darby instinctively held Sissy closer, her throat tightening with emotion.

"*Who could have known that such tragedy could lead to a new life, a new love?*"

A shot of Darby's New York condo loomed into focus.

"*It was here, in the heart of Long Island, that the story really begins.*"

More grainy photographs of Darby's deck, her lobby, her doorman.

"*Six weeks ago, Darby Simms couldn't have known that she would be on the brink of marriage.*"

"You can say that again," Darby muttered under her breath.

"*Until that time, she worked as an assistant to Ricardo Yvonne, the exclusive fashion designer. She hadn't a care in the world.*"

"I wouldn't say that," Darby commented. She'd been given a three-week vacation from work for "honeymoon" purposes, but she didn't dare take that long. If she did, a half dozen up-and-coming employees at Ricardo Yvonne would be after her job—and she didn't trust Ricardo not to supplant her if he experienced a moment of panic when forced to speak personally with his suppliers.

"Then, in the middle of the night, a bouncing bundle of joy was left on her doorstep."

Darby's brows rose. In reality, it had been four in the afternoon and the baby had been delivered by Eloise's ex-housekeeper. In a half-dozen guttural, German-laced sentences, the woman had informed Darby of Eloise's death, then had proceeded to add that Darby had been named as executor of Eloise's will. According to the document, all of Eloise's worldly goods—as well as the million-dollar Nashton china fortune—were to be kept in trust for baby Sharece until such time as the infant could be united with her natural father.

"Who could have known that such an infant, already an heiress, could have united Darby Simms with the love of her life, Chauncey LeRoy Fitch?"

Darby grimaced. Calling the man "the love of her life" bordered on the realm of fiction. But then, even "The Gossip Exchange" couldn't have known that Eloise had died before finishing her will. Otherwise, Darby wouldn't have been forced to serve as amateur detective in order to discover just who Sharece's father had been. As it was, she'd had to read her friend's diary, make a list of possible paternity "candidates,'' then track down their current where-abouts.

Luckily for her, the first man she'd interviewed, Chauncey Fitch, had admitted quite candidly that he was Eloise's lover and the baby's father.

Unfortunately, by that time Darby had grown quite attached to the child. When she had voiced her reservations to having the baby cared for by a nanny because of Chauncey's frequent absences from home, he'd suggested a ''marriage of convenience.'' She could continue to care for the baby, legally and morally. In exchange, he would gain a mother for his daughter and a full-time hostess for entertaining his business partners.

''. . . What ensued was a whirlwind courtship and a fairy-tale wedding.''

Darby rolled her eyes. In truth, what had ensued was a meeting with Chauncey's lawyers for a prenuptial agreement, then a visit to his mother's palatial town house—where *she* had already made all the plans.

Growling in disgust, Darby shut the television off, flooding the room with silence.

Sissy, who had been watching the kaleidoscope of colors dancing in front of her, glanced up and threw Darby a frown. Then, when she saw she had Darby's full attention, she grinned.

''You think this is funny, don't you, Sissy?''

Sissy's arms flailed in agreement and she offered a giggle that dissolved into a fit of bubble blowing.

''That's only because you don't have to wear this ghastly outfit.''

Nor do you have to marry a stranger.

As soon as the thought crystallized, Darby pushed it away. There was no sense thinking that way. She'd been given plenty of time to make a decision about wedding Chauncey Fitch. She'd reviewed all aspects of the "merger" calmly and rationally. And after insisting that her own rights be protected should *she* be the one to terminate the marriage, she'd found no reason not to go through with the whole—

The whole three-ring circus!

Darby grinned when her own inner voice chimed in to finish the sentence—for there was no other way to describe the ceremony. She and Chauncey were to be married in The Wedding Forum's elaborate formal garden beneath an awning of ivory striped damask.

"I'm even wearing the clown outfit," Darby muttered and Sissy chortled right on cue, reaching for the headdress made of ruffled tulle with its chenille trim—chenille, for heaven's sake. Darby had always thought that particular fuzzy sort of fringe was reserved for bathrobes.

Darby was about to follow her statement with a round of "bugaboo" prattle and a flurry of tickles to Sissy's stomach, when the door burst open and Ida rushed inside. Behind her Chauncey's Aunt Patty was blotting her flushed cheeks with a handkerchief.

"He's here! He's here!" Aunt Patty exclaimed before Ida could speak, her chubby face florid with the exertion it had taken for her to run from the front foyer where she'd been keeping vigil.

Ida threw the woman a scowl of warning and added, "We've got to hurry, there's another wedding scheduled at five, so they want us out of here in an hour."

Out in an hour? Gee, so much for atmosphere, for memories, for...

Darby squelched her conscience's instinctive reaction to the situation.

Ida plucked Sissy from Darby's arms and scooped up the diaper bag from the floor. Then she gestured to Darby. "Come along, dear."

Darby didn't immediately respond. Now that the moment had come for her to rendezvous with her husband-to-be, she couldn't quite summon the enthusiasm that she knew she should feel.

"Darby," Ida chided.

Burying another sigh, Darby stood and waited patiently as Patty fluffed her skirt and arranged her veil. Once again, the scent of mothballs hovered around her like an ill wind.

You mean like a stinkin' cloud of doom. Just like the green mist in Cecil B. DeMille's Ten Commandments. *The guests will take one whiff of you and—*

Stop it! Darby silently chided herself, wondering why her voice had become so insistent lately, offering comments and suggestions at will.

Darby trailed Ida out of the Bridal Room and down a long corridor to where a pair of French doors opened into the gardens. There, the path had been covered with yards of ivory sateen, which led past the rosebushes and perennial beds, through the rows of guests, to the awning and the altar.

"You wait here, with Darby," Ida ordered Aunt Patty, handing her the baby. "I'll signal the orchestra and the bridesmaids."

There were twelve bridesmaids—an inordinate amount in Darby's opinion, especially since she didn't know any of them personally. Evidently Ida had saved all of the gowns from her own bridal party, and she'd insisted that each of them be put to use.

"Once you hear the wedding march, that will be your signal to step into view."

Yeah, yeah, Darby's inner voice answered sarcastically, but outwardly, Darby summoned her best smile. A smile that felt stiff and awkward.

Patty sniffled, juggling the baby into the crook of one arm as she reached for the handkerchief tucked into her belt.

"I'm so happy," she said between hiccuping sighs. "You've made us all so happy."

Patty impulsively threw one arm around Darby's shoulder and hugged her close. "After Chauncey's bout with mumps made him sterile all those years ago, I never thought he'd marry. Yet, here you are, willing to overlook that detail. And in the process, you've given me more than I could have ever hoped for—a little grandniece."

Then she was whirling away and rushing outdoors.

Leaving Darby stunned. Frozen.

As she waited for her cue, one single word kept reverberating through her head.

Sterile... sterile... sterile...

CHRISTIAN DRAKE swore as the wheel to his '57 Studebaker pulled sharply to the right and he heard the betraying *fluppita-fluppita* noise, which could only mean that one of his tires had gone flat.

Maneuvering the car to the curb, he applied the brakes and coasted to a halt.

"Damn," he muttered under his breath. Not bothering to open the door, he vaulted out of the convertible and rounded the hood just as a limousine came barreling over the steep hill and screeched to a stop mere inches behind him.

"Hey!" he called to the tall, blond man who emerged from the back seat without waiting for his driver to open his door. "Don't you think you've parked a little close, pal?"

The stranger didn't pause. "I'm late, I'm *late!*" he shouted, pointing to the imposing building.

It was then that Christian noted the discreet, hand-lettered sign that had been pounded into the middle of the verdant grass. *The Marriage Forum.* From there, his gaze slid to the chauffeur who had emerged from the limousine and was calmly stringing a length of ribbon from the hood ornament to the sideview mirror.

The sight was enough to spur Christian into action. Not only did he want to avoid being in the path of the soon-to-be newlyweds' getaway car, but he also didn't want to get this close to marriage. Anyone's marriage. The mere memory of his own short sojourn into that institution was enough to make him shudder.

Taking his keys from the dashboard, he popped the trunk and took out the jack and the spare, his actions quick and practiced. As he began to pump the front end of the car off the ground, he freely admitted to himself that his reaction to having a wedding chapel a few yards away was overblown, but he didn't care. His first and only marriage had been an utter disaster. Granted, he'd been eighteen when he'd eloped, and his high-school sweetheart had trapped him into the situation by telling him she was pregnant—a minor detail which had proven to be untrue.

Nevertheless, the experience had taught him that women might be beautiful to hold, but there was a whole other nightmare waiting in the wings if a man was stupid enough to get caught in a permanent situation. The moodiness, the cobweb of nylons over the shower door, the preoccupation with babies and small animals. A few weeks of such inanities was enough to drive even the hardest man mad—especially one who'd spent the past two years isolated from civilization in the Amazon Rain Forest.

As he removed the flat tire and replaced it with the spare, he grimaced. After enduring twenty-four months of heat, humidity, insects and rodents, while supervising the construction of a bridge over a tributary of the Amazon, he'd vowed that he would take a year off, tour the country in his vintage car, follow whatever whim possessed him. And now, less than fifty miles from his original destination, he'd been delayed by his first obstacle.

He winced when the strains of the wedding march sifted through the air, bringing with it the images of a bride who had been more interested in Christian's checkbook than in building a life together.

He had to get out of here. Now.

SHE HAD TO GET OUT of here. Now.

Darby heard the opening bars to the wedding march, and a part of her took an instinctive step forward. From some distant place, she acknowledged the elderly Forum employee who handed her a huge bouquet jammed with camellias, roses and ivy. She even noted the two dozen doves, which had been released and the gasps of the audience as they caught their first glimpse of the bride.

But what caught and held her attention was Patty Fitch and the infant she held in her arms.

Sterile. *Sterile.* Chauncey Fitch was sterile. He'd had the mumps.

A hysterical giggle threatened to push from her throat, but she tamped it down through sheer will, staring at the man destined to become her groom.

No wonder he'd been so comfortable with the prospect of a marriage of convenience. No wonder he had never kissed her—never even broached the subject. No wonder he'd dodged her questions about future children. He didn't plan to *give* her children. Ever. Naturally she'd assumed that once they'd grown to care for each other, that there might be a chance...that he and she might...that they would...

Do the bedroom mambo? her little voice mocked.

Physically, she supposed that being sterile, he could still...launch the rocket, so to speak. But there could never be a tangible product from such intimacies.

He'd been telling the truth when he'd said that he wanted her only as a mother for his child and a hostess for his—

His child. *His?*

That sneaky, lying, no-good—

Bastard. Go ahead and admit it. He's a bastard. He doesn't really want you or the kid. What he wants is the Nashton million.

The truth hit her like a thunderbolt, midway up the aisle.

No wonder Chauncey had made no effort to become accustomed to Sissy. He'd claimed he had to work long hours in order to be able to take time off for the wedding, but now that Darby thought about it, he'd spent more time bonding with the figures in the baby's bank account than he ever had with the child herself. Even his mother had been stiff and unresponsive around the baby. She was probably privy to the whole sordid mess. If it hadn't been for his aunt, Darby might never have known the truth.

Damn him. How dare he toy with Sissy's life? With Darby's!

Darby met Chauncey's benign smile with a glare. She must have been close enough to the altar for him to read her expression, because his own placid mien faltered. His brows lifted questioningly.

Darby's anger multiplied with each step she took—as did her speed. What had begun as a numbed procession up the aisle, grew quicker and quicker, until she was nearly running and the orchestra was struggling to keep up with the pace.

Finally she stopped at Chauncey's side. As she looked at this man who had lied to her, who had tampered with Sissy's future, who had been willing to live a lie for money, she could scarcely contain her anger.

Chauncey reached for Darby's hand.

"Dearly Beloved," the pastor intoned.

"You bastard," Darby growled in a low whisper.

The pastor's jaw dropped.

Chauncey flushed.

"You lied to me, Chauncey."

His eyes moved from side to side and he murmured out of the corner of his mouth, "Not now. Whatever it is can wait."

"Mumps."

The one word received more attention from this man than she'd had all week.

"Darby, I can explain everything."

She noticed immediately that he didn't bother to deny that he'd lied to her.

"You *aren't* Sissy's father."

He shook his head.

"Then we have nothing more to discuss." She thrust the bouquet into Chauncey's arms.

The pastor's eyes threatened to pop from his head.

"I'm sorry, pastor, but this ceremony will not be taking place."

Chapter Two

Darby tore the headpiece from her hair. Behind her, she heard a collective gasp from the audience. "Goodbye, Chauncey."

Lifting the scratchy net skirts out of her way, Darby ran from the canopy-covered altar, her sights trained on one thing. Sissy. Already, the guests were beginning to murmur, shifting uncomfortably in their seats. Instinctively Darby knew that she only had a few moments to escape. If she didn't, someone was bound to stop her, to force an explanation or a re-evaluation of her decision.

She had to get out of here!

Hiking her skirts even higher, she dashed in Patty Fitch's direction, all but wrenched the baby out of her arms, then scooped the diaper bag from where it had been hidden out of sight at the woman's side. All the while, she thanked whatever Fates had inspired her to tuck her wallet and a few necessary items into the bag.

"I'm sorry, Patty," Darby gasped. True, she'd never had a chance to become very well acquainted with the woman, but Patty had been genuinely taken with Sissy. "I know you want a grandniece, but I can't do this. It would be a horrible, horrible mistake." Backing away, she yelled in Ida's direction, "I'll see that the dress gets back to you, I promise."

Then Darby was running down the aisle, dodging the hands that were already trying to stop her. She shot past the openmouthed employees of the Forum, through the graceful archways of the inner corridors and out the front door.

Once she'd reached the wide, curved portico, she stopped, gasping for breath. She didn't have a car, she realized abruptly.

She didn't have a car!

Wide-eyed, she searched for some avenue of escape, knowing that if she didn't hurry, the Fitches would be upon her—or worse yet, the media personnel who had been invited to cover the ceremony for the local papers and television stations.

But even as she searched, she saw nothing that could help her. Nothing but the limousine being polished by Chauncey's chauffeur and...

And a lean, dark-haired stranger throwing a tire into the back of a vintage convertible.

Without pausing to think things through, Darby ran toward the stranger. As he bent to pick up the jack he'd laid on the curb next to the trunk, she threw the diaper bag into the back seat.

The snap of the passenger-side latch alerted the man and he slammed the trunk shut. "Hey! What do you think you're doing?"

"Just get in," she ordered, glancing over her shoulder.

The front door of The Forum flew open and Chauncey dashed out. "Darby! Darby, get back here! I can explain."

The stranger's eyes darted from Darby, to Sissy, then to Chauncey. "What the hell . . ."

"Get in and drive!" Darby urgently pleaded. "Please, just get in and drive."

Some small part of her desperation must have communicated itself to the man, because he rounded the back of the vehicle and vaulted into the driver's seat.

"Where are we going?"

"Anywhere."

Chauncey was getting closer. Only a few yards separated them now.

The stranger took one last look at the prospective groom, reached for the key and revved the engine. "Fine. Whatever you say."

Then he was screeching away from the curb, leaving Chauncey to yell in vain, *"Daaaarby! Come baaaack!"*

CHRISTIAN WASN'T SURE why he'd allowed his instincts to take over. He was usually a private person, a cautious person—a byproduct of his career, he supposed, since such qualities were useful when it involved erecting bridges in primitive surroundings. Normally he wouldn't have accepted a stranger as a passenger.

But this was no normal situation. One look at the woman ensconced in the seat beside him was all he needed to reassure him of that fact.

Her delicate features were tense, her lips pursed. Her grip on the infant was tight enough for even the baby to squirm. Nevertheless, Christian waited until they were well away from the Wedding Forum before asking, "So what do you want me to do now?"

The woman at his side was still glancing over her shoulder from time to time, as if she expected a fleet of squad cars to overtake them at any moment.

"Just keep driving."

"Which way?"

"Anywhere," she muttered, then corrected herself. "Head east. Join the interstate and head east."

Christian shrugged, but since the woman's demands were in keeping with his original plans, he didn't argue. Instead he did his best to maneuver his way through the city until he could navigate the appropriate on-ramp. Then, when the wind was blowing through their hair and they were maintaining a cruising speed, he looked at her again.

The whole situation was so preposterous, he knew he should laugh. He had just been hijacked by a bride and a baby. The front seat of his car was crowded with a puff of some horrible fabric that caught the breeze and blew against his arm in an annoying manner, while an infant stared up at him with wide, dark eyes as if he were some sort of alien.

"Whose kid?" he asked, deciding he should at least inquire about the baby in case he'd become an accomplice to an abduction.

"Mine."

"You're sure?"

She glared at him. "Yes, I'm sure."

She seemed serious enough, so he let the matter drop.

"You're not going to make me go back to San Francisco, are you?" he asked after they'd endured several minutes of silence.

"No."

Again, he was riddled with questions. So where *did* she plan to go? Who was she? And why had she run away from her own wedding, only to take refuge with a stranger?

"Is there anything illegal going on here?" he demanded.

Again, she scowled at him, her eyes flashing. He was struck then by their unusual color. He'd never seen anyone with eyes so pale green, like sagebrush in the summer. And her hair was a sun-streaked blond, short, tousled and infinitely appealing.

"No. There is nothing illegal going on here."

He studied her more thoroughly, taking in the rigid set of her features—delicate features enhanced by great bone structure. The wind whipped at her hair, giving her the appearance of some sort of waif playing dress-up in her mother's clothes. His gaze dropped to her bare shoulders and the strapless bodice of her gown. No, he'd have to take that idea back. She was no waif. Her body was far from childlike and curved in all the right places.

He allowed another few minutes to pass before saying, "I think you owe me some sort of explanation."

Her jaw tensed as if she were clenching her teeth.

"After all, I could be in danger."

Her gaze flew in his direction.

"You might be some sort of felon, or a bank robber on the run."

His teasing paid off, because her lips curved ever so slightly.

"I assure you, nothing that exotic is happening here."

"Then what?" he prompted. "Don't tell me you're some sort of escaped prisoner."

That caused her mouth to twist in self-deprecation. "That description might suit this matter."

He waited, knowing that she was on the verge of some sort of confession.

"I... ran away from my own wedding."

"No kidding," he said sarcastically.

A small laugh burst from her lips. "I guess that *was* stating the obvious, wasn't it?"

"I'd say so."

He saw the way her white-knuckled grip on the infant eased.

She took a shuddering breath. "I'm not going back."

"No one said you had to."

Again, she inhaled, exhaled, then slouched in her seat as if she were suddenly exhausted. "Where are you going?"

"Lake Tahoe."

Her brows lifted in surprise. "Really?"

"I'm on vacation."

She bit her lower lip in indecision. "Can I go with you?"

Christian was sure he'd heard her incorrectly. "You want to go to Tahoe?"

"Yes."

"Why?"

"Because I can't go back there."

Christian felt a curious twisting sensation in his gut.

"Did someone hurt you?"

She shook her head. "No. But they lied to me, and in my book that's just as bad."

Christian saw the anger rise in her eyes and didn't press for more information. Especially since he could commiserate with her. He'd endured enough lies concerning his own ill-fated wedding to fill a book.

"It'll be hours before we even get to Nevada. You can't go like that." He gestured to her dress.

She'd obviously caught his unconscious "we" because her body lost most of its remaining tension.

"You'll let us go with you?"

He hesitated. He'd been given no real explanations. At least none to reassure himself that he wasn't becoming embroiled in some sort of messy domestic situation. But somehow, instinctively, he knew he couldn't refuse this woman. Not when she so obviously needed his help.

Since she was still waiting for his answer, he shrugged. "Why not?" His gaze flicked to her bare shoulders. "But I think you'll want to wear something else. It will get cold later."

She sighed. "I've got the baby's things, but most of mine were left behind."

"You're sure you don't want to go back and get them?"

She shook her head. "I've deserted jeans and shirts, some toiletries. They can all be replaced. But if you've got time, I would appreciate it if you could stop at some sort of department store so I can get something else."

Ordinarily, Christian would have been irritated. He was one of those travelers who did things on *his* schedule. Once he set his mind to be somewhere, he wanted to be there with the least amount of fuss possible.

But, he reminded himself, he was on vacation. He had all the time in the world. And for some odd reason, this woman's request didn't irritate him in the least.

Especially since he thought they would all be better off if Miss-Whatever-Her-Name-Was covered her shoulders and the sweet upper curves of her breasts.

HE STOPPED just on the outer limits of Oakland. But when he twisted in his seat, he realized that she couldn't go walking around in that dress. Not without creating a good deal of attention.

"I think you'd better give me a list of what you want."

She must have come to the same realization about her attire, because she looked relieved.

"Thanks."

Reaching for the diaper bag, she withdrew a well-worn day-planner, then sighed when the zipper fastener proved awkward to maneuver with one hand.

"Here, you hold the baby."

"Me?"

"She won't bite."

Christian wasn't so sure about that. The infant was sleeping, but he'd been around a few babies in his lifetime—well, three. In his experience, they screamed, they pooped and they gnawed on things. That was about all they were good for.

"Please?"

Knowing that he would be interpreted as some sort of ogre if he didn't hold the kid, Christian held his arms out straight, accepting the weight of the infant.

"Tuck her against your chest."

"Her?" For the first time, the gender of the baby caught his attention. Great. A girl. He knew even less about how to handle girls.

"Yes. Her name is Sissy."

He tore his gaze away from the baby to stare at the woman hovering so protectively near. Didn't she know that by bending close she afforded Christian a splendid view of her cleavage and the velvety texture of her skin?

"Don't you think I should know your name, too?"

Her reluctance was obvious.

"Come on," he urged. "I promise I won't turn you in."

Her smile was fleeting and somewhat sad. "I told you, I haven't done anything illegal."

"Then it couldn't hurt for me to know your name."

"Darby. Darby Simms."

"Christian Drake."

She nodded uncomfortably, and since he wanted to smooth over the awkward moment, he said, "Go ahead with your list. I don't know how long Sissy will let me hold her. As soon as she gets one good look at me, she'll probably scream."

Darby scribbled a few things onto one of the calendar pages, ripped it free, then handed him the paper along with a credit card.

"Just sign my name on the receipt."

"You're sure?"

She nodded. "If there are any problems I can clear the charges with my bank when I notify them later on."

Darby took the baby from him then, leaning so close to Christian that he could smell the sweet scent clinging to her hair.

When she'd settled into her place, he left with some reluctance. For the first time since she'd commandeered his services, she was looking very vulnerable and unsure.

"You'll be all right while I'm gone?"

"Yes, but hurry. Your car attracts enough attention. I don't want to be the cause of any more. I'd rather blend into the woodwork."

As Christian made his way to the front entrance, he doubted Darby Simms could ever blend into the woodwork. Not with that body.

Not with that face.

IT SEEMED LIKE an eternity had passed before Darby saw Christian Drake pushing a heavily laden cart through the sliding doors. His short, wavy hair gleamed chocolate brown in the sunlight and she knew already that his eyes would be just as dark and rich.

"He's coming, Sissy," she whispered, smoothing the fuzz on the baby's head.

Sissy didn't respond other than to snuggle more firmly into Darby's arms and sleep.

Darby heard the rattle of the steel wheels from some distance, but even if she hadn't, she would have known that Christian was near. A tingling began at her nape and radiated through her body as if she had been infused with some sort of electric charge.

"Here are the things you needed."

His voice had the subtle rumble of a distant storm.

"Are you sure you wanted me to get a car seat?"

"Yes." She gently lay the baby on the cushions next to her, propping the diaper bag by her side so Sissy wouldn't roll into harm's way. "She can't go all the way to Tahoe without some sort of safety precautions. Especially in a convertible."

He shrugged as if to say that it was no big deal to him what she did with her money. Little did he know that she had more funds than he could imagine at her disposal. Eloise's lawyers had insisted on being quite generous with distributing a monthly stipend for Sissy's personal needs.

Climbing from the car, she helped Christian take the car seat from the box and install it in the back seat of the Studebaker. Then, she grabbed a pair of jeans from the sack, tore off the tags and stepped into them, pulling them up to her hips.

Christian stuffed the tips of his fingers into his pockets and glanced around them at the other shoppers making their way to the store.

"You're going to change out here?"

"Only the skirt."

Darby reached for the catch at the back of the net, thanking heaven above that the bustier was not permanently attached. If it had been, she would have been forced to disrobe in the store rest room most likely. She didn't even want to think of the attention she would have garnered making her way inside.

Darby stuffed the yards and yards of white net into the floor space behind the front seat. Delving into the sack again, she removed an oversize, red T-shirt and dragged it over the satin bustier, then raked her fingers through her hair.

"Did you get sunglasses?"

"In the other bag."

She searched through a sack laden with toiletries and fished out the sunglasses.

"What's this?" she asked, gesturing to a bag of cheese puffs.

"Lunch. Don't worry, I paid for it myself. They must have put it in the wrong sack."

She gazed at him askance, studying his trim physique—no, not just trim. Sculpted. Athletic.

"You eat this to look like—" her hand waved at him indiscriminately "—that?"

"Like what?"

She wasn't about to explain. She didn't think she could.

Not without sounding like some randy teenager.

"You look healthy."

"So?"

"So I would have thought you'd eat that way, too."

He grabbed the bag. "What isn't healthy about it?" He circled in the direction of the driver's door. "It has cheese."

"Yeah, right."

"Well, it has cheese flavor. That's good enough for me."

Taking his place, he waited while she set the baby in the car seat and then arranged a makeshift canopy over the baby's face by draping a receiving blanket over the carrying handle. Fortunately the weather was mild, but she didn't want to chance too much exposure to the elements—and after all the demands she'd already made, she didn't dare ask if the vehicle had a top.

"All set?" he asked once she'd fastened her own seat belt.

"Sure."

The car purred out of the parking lot.

"I've got to stop and get a tire repaired before we get under way," Christian informed her. "Is that going to be a problem?"

"I'm in no hurry."

But you are. You want to get out of here. You want to put this place behind you.

Darby rubbed her temples, feeling the beginnings of an ache settle behind her eyes. Now that she was away from the hoopla of the wedding and all its worries, she realized that it had been weeks since she'd really slept. Her nights had been restless and filled with what-ifs for the future. Moreover, she was starving, absolutely starving.

Without asking permission, she dug her hand into the bag of cheese puffs.

Christian glanced at her briefly, then returned his attention to the road. "I thought you didn't approve of my choice in junk food."

"I don't."

He chuckled. "Then help yourself. There's more goodies in one of the bags on the back seat."

Reaching into the back seat, she snagged the plastic sack. Inside was a plethora of supplies—a six-pack of cola, boxes of juice, beef jerky, string cheese, M&M's, sunflower seeds, crackers, tortilla chips and a jar of salsa.

"You've got quite a...selection," she commented, choosing some juice, cheese and a handful of crackers.

"I've been out of the country."

"Oh, really?" She eyed him more closely. Suddenly it struck her that she didn't know anything about this man. She might rue the day she'd manipulated him into helping her.

But even as the thought formed, Darby dismissed it. She trusted him. She didn't know why, but she did. From the moment she'd seen him throwing his tire into the trunk, there had been an intangible sense of recognition on her part, as if she'd met this man somewhere.

"Where are you from?" she asked, determined to get to the bottom of the unusual emotions she was experiencing in his presence.

"I was born in Kansas."

You're both from the Midwest, her little voice said. *So what? That doesn't make him trustworthy.*

But since she'd begun her interrogation, she might as well finish. "What do you do for a living?"

"I build bridges."

Her eyes widened. "Why?"

He opened his mouth as if he were about to offer a pat answer, paused, then chuckled. "No one's ever asked me that question before."

"I like to know what makes people tick."

"Why?"

She grinned at his own quick retort. "Before she died, my mother once told me that I had an old soul. I am far too curious about the people I meet. I want to know what motivates them, what interests them."

"You must have been a psychology major."

"What makes you think I've been to college?"

"You radiate intelligence" was the only answer he gave, but when she regarded him suspiciously, he pointed to the ring she wore on her right hand. "I recognized the insignia for the Sorbonne. They don't give those out at the dime store."

Her brows rose even more. He had a keen eye and an attention for detail.

"I also noticed you aren't wearing an engagement ring. Did you throw it at his feet?"

"Whose?"

"Your groom's."

She rubbed her bare wedding-ring finger. "No. I never had a ring."

"Curiouser and curiouser."

"Chauncey never had the time to choose one. I see now that he never bothered to take the time."

"Chauncey who?"

"Fitch."

"Funny, you don't look like someone who would become a 'Mrs. Fitch.'"

"You know the Fitches?"

"No, I was speaking generally." There was a beat of silence. "*Were* you a psychology major?"

She shook her head. "Fashion."

"You don't sound French."

"I'm from Iowa. I went to the Sorbonne on scholarship."

He whistled lowly. "That's some scholarship."

Darby didn't bother to elaborate that the scholarship had been funded by the Nashton China Works, yet another reason why she felt indebted to carrying out Eloise's wishes. Eloise had done so much for Darby that she felt a deep-rooted obligation to see to it that Sissy was reunited with her biological father.

So why did the thought hurt so much? Why did the prospect of turning Sissy over to a stranger cause her heart to throb? The baby had only been in Darby's care for a few short weeks. Why, then, did she feel that Sissy was hers—*hers*—as much as if the baby had been her own flesh and blood? It was doubtful that the next candidate would offer a solution of marriage so that Darby could be near the infant. If Eloise's wishes were going to be honored, Darby would have to let the little girl go.

Her eyes squeezed closed as she fought for calm.

Somehow, she would have to find the strength to do the right thing.

Even if it broke her heart in the process.

Chapter Three

Christian turned the car into a service station, causing Darby to pay more attention to their surroundings. A dingy garage, the odor of grease and hulking piles of new tires.

"I'm going to fill the tank with gas." After pulling to a stop, Christian glanced over his shoulder at the baby. "Will the fumes bother her?"

"Not with this breeze."

He was about to get out of the car when she touched his forearm. Its warmth and strength surprised her, as did the crisp texture of the hair that dusted his skin.

"Mr. Drake, I have to ask..."

"Yes," he prompted when she hesitated.

"You wouldn't do anything to hurt Sissy, would you?"

She saw the way he started at the mere idea. "Hell, no."

"Then I can trust you to take us to Lake Tahoe?"

His eyes narrowed. "Why? Why are you so willing to come with me? You're not broke, are you? Was that credit card maxed out?"

She shook her head. "I'm afraid if I used the normal means of transportation, my departure would become fodder for the media." She shuddered to think what "The Gossip Exchange" would make of today's events, but since she would be unable to prevent some sort of reaction, it was imperative that she avoid any further publicity, if possible. Since there was no way that Chauncey could have been Sissy's father, she had five more candidates to investigate—and one of them lived in Utah. If she could get as far as Nevada, she could go the rest of the way by plane or bus. By avoiding any news coverage, she could ensure that the next candidate had no forewarning of Sissy's arrival.

"What does the media have to do with all this?" Christian asked.

Darby chose her words carefully. "My ex-fiancé was a well-known businessman."

It was apparent from his expression that he thought she was withholding a good deal of information, but he didn't pry any further.

"I'll just take care of the tire."

Darby watched him as he jumped onto the pavement, then made his way to the office of the service department. As he did, she couldn't help wishing that Sissy's father, whoever he might be, would prove to be just as decent and honorable as this guy had been. After all, he hadn't rescued one damsel in distress.

He'd rescued two.

CHRISTIAN GRUNTED in response to the chatting service station attendant as the man replaced the inner tube and prattled on and on about old cars. Normally Christian would have been in his heyday conversing with someone who had more than the average person's automotive know-how. But at the moment, he was too distracted to think about anyone but Darby Simms.

Had he gone crazy? What was he doing traveling to Tahoe with a bride and a baby? It didn't make sense. People didn't just jump into other people's cars and finagle a ride to Nevada. For all he knew, she could be stark-raving mad herself.

Sighing, he dismissed the thought. She wasn't nuts. When she'd spoken to him, her eyes had blazed with the same protectiveness a lioness might show her cub. He had no doubts that she was serious in her intent to leave the area. If Christian didn't help her, she would find another way.

So that left him with his original question. Why *was* he helping her? If his colleagues could see him now, Christian knew he would have become the butt of some good-natured ribbing. On the job site, he'd gained the nickname "Iron Man." Not because of his abilities or physique, but because he had a reputation for refusing the advances of the ladies. He was a confirmed bachelor. A loner. A...

"There y'go, mister."

Christian jumped, then followed the man into the inner office to pay. As he went, he chided himself for his inattention.

Keep your mind on the road ahead, he reminded himself. Judging by her dash from the wedding chapel, this woman was hip-deep in trouble. If he involved himself in her affairs, he couldn't escape being dragged into her problems as well.

"So," Christian said once they were well under way and he'd finished half of the cheese puffs. "Why are you on your way to Tahoe with me instead of sipping champagne with your groom?"

"It's a long story."

"We've got plenty of time."

Darby considered telling Christian everything, the way she'd suddenly been put in charge of a child, the search for Sissy's father, the mess with Chauncey Fitch. But she stopped herself before she could surrender to such an indulgence. She would be separating from Christian Drake's company as soon as they arrived in Tahoe, so there was no use burdening him with her life story or the baby's.

"I'd rather skip it, if you don't mind."

"Fine."

But the tone of his voice was far from reassuring.

He's going to end up asking you again. You know he will.

But she didn't care. Right now, all that mattered was getting out of San Francisco with Sissy before the media made a heyday out of the wedding debacle and ruined all chances of finding the baby's real father. There were still five more candidates to investigate. Five men who had spent time with Eloise Nashton nine months before her daughter was born—and since

Eloise had never mentioned intimate details about her sex life, there was no way to tell which one had made love to her.

Darby tucked her appointment book more firmly into the diaper bag. Inside, she'd made a list of the eligible bachelors: Nick Rassmussen of Utah, an ex-Olympic skier turned land developer; Alec Davinci of Indiana, race-car driver; Lucien DuBois of Louisiana, philanthropist; Collin West of Kentucky, horse breeder; and Compton Smythe of Virginia, research clinician.

All of them would have to be interviewed and carefully screened, but this time, Darby would have to be more careful.

This time, she would have to make sure that none of them were after the baby for her money.

THEY WERE TWO HOURS outside of Los Angeles when Christian first suspected that something was wrong with Darby Simms. She'd grown increasingly quiet with each mile they drove, and looking at her now, he saw that her head had dropped back against the seat and her lashes formed shadows against her skin. Pale skin. Very pale skin. Almost . . . green.

"Are you all right?"

"Fine."

But the answer was garbled.

"You don't look fine."

"No, really, I'm . . ."

He wouldn't have thought it possible, but she grew even more pallid.

"Pull over," she croaked.

He didn't wait for a second bidding. It was obvious that she wasn't well.

Pulling onto the shoulder, he eased to a stop. The wheels were still crunching on the gravel when she pushed open the door and hurried to a mound of straggling bushes. She didn't empty her stomach as Christian had thought she would. Instead she leaned one hand against a fence post and took deep breaths of the cool air. Several minutes later, she returned, staggering slightly.

"You're ill," Christian stated needlessly.

"No kidding," she said with a groan, then flashed him an apologetic smile. "Sorry, I'm a real grump when I'm nauseous."

"Are you carsick?"

She glowered at him as if the idea itself was preposterous. "I doubt it. This isn't motion sickness. This isn't the flu. This is—" she pressed a hand to her stomach as if it were roiling, then added uncomfortably "—bad food."

The instant the statement left her mouth, their gazes connected. Leaning over the seat, Christian snagged the sack of munchies. He examined the cheese. Nothing. The crackers. Nothing. The juice.

He grimaced. "The expiration date on this juice is two years ago."

Darby moaned and sank into her seat, but when she tried to close the heavy door, she didn't have the strength.

Christian leaned past her, ignoring the potent heat of her feverish body, and tugged on the handle until the latch clicked.

"Can you hold on until the next town?"

She shook her head. "Tahoe. Take me to Tahoe."

"You'll never make it."

She shot him a stern look. "I've already disrupted your schedule more than I ever should have. I won't trouble you any further."

He wanted to tell her that she was no trouble, not really, but she'd closed her eyes and laid her head against the seat again.

Pushing on the accelerator, he eased into traffic, then edged his speed slightly over the limit. If Darby wanted to go to Tahoe, fine. But he'd see to it that they got there as soon and as safely as possible.

Meanwhile, he thought as he cast a look at the baby in the back seat, he could only pray that Missy... Chrissie... Prissy... the *kid* ... continued to sleep to the hum of the tires. He didn't relish having to deal with her should she awaken.

He hadn't been lying when he'd told Darby that he had no experience with babies.

CHRISTIAN EASED HIS CAR into a parking place next to a small hotel just outside Lake Tahoe's city limits. In the valley below, the lake glimmered in the moonlight like a huge puddle of ink. Around it lay the scattered jewels made by the city lights.

They'd made good time to Nevada. Thankfully the baby *had* slept most of the way—as had her mother—but Sissy was growing fretful, and he was sure that the feeding she'd received two hours ago was beginning to wear off.

He glanced down at the woman curled up in the passenger seat. Darby's legs were drawn beneath her and her hands were tucked under one cheek. In that pose, with the stillness of slumber relaxing her delicate features, she looked like a child herself. So vulnerable, so sweet. She certainly didn't look like a mother—not that Christian supposed there was any sort of a stereotype to such a vocation, but he had always thought the experience would add a certain maturity to one's face.

"Darby?"

He touched her shoulder and she groaned, drawing away from him and causing the fabric of her shirt to pull against one breast, reminding him all too clearly that she still wore the satin bustier beneath.

"We're here."

Her lashes flickered and she blearily surveyed the illuminated parking lot bordered with simple, cinder-block buildings.

"Where?" she croaked.

Behind her, the baby whimpered and Darby squeezed her eyes closed as if the sound pained her.

Christian didn't know the precise moment he'd made his decision to watch over this woman until she was feeling better. It might have been the last time she'd struggled to feed the baby while doing her best to control her own unsettled stomach. It might have been when she'd succumbed to her illness and spent twenty minutes in a rest area bathroom vomiting. In any event, it didn't matter. He couldn't leave her alone. Not like this.

"Stay here," he ordered.

He wasn't sure if she even heard him. Her head had lolled against the seat again, and she was reaching behind her to feebly rock the car seat in an effort to calm the baby.

Knowing he only had a few minutes before the baby would start to scream, he strode into the office, arranged for a room, then returned and drove to the appropriate ground-floor abode.

Darby hadn't even stirred. Her eyes remained closed, her skin so white he could see the tracery of veins at her temples. If not for the way she mechanically jiggled the baby seat, he would have thought she was unconscious.

It took him nearly ten minutes to unstrap Sissy from the safety seat. By that time, she was staring at him with tear-filled eyes, her lower lip trembling, whimpers of distress bubbling from her throat.

At long last, Christian freed her and managed to carry her in the crook of his arm, his free hand grasping the diaper bag, shopping bags and his own duffel bag. There were two double beds, and he set the baby in the middle of the mattress closest to the bathroom. Then he returned to the car for Darby.

"Come on." He pulled open her door.

She was still jiggling the empty car seat.

Smothering a grin that he knew she wouldn't appreciate, he scooped her into his arms.

"What are you doing?"

"I'm putting you to bed."

One of her eyes opened and, this time, he couldn't suppress a chuckle. "Don't worry. I'm not about to make any sort of move you aren't likely to appreciate.''

This time, both eyes stared his way.

Laughing again, he carried her into the motel room and set her next to the baby.

''I have . . . to feed . . . Sissy.''

He pushed her down when she attempted to rise.

''Sleep. I think I can figure out which end is up as far as the baby is concerned.'' Even as the words left his mouth, he prayed he could live up to them.

But as Darby rolled onto her side and drew her knees against her chest, he wondered if he'd spoken too soon. The baby had begun to cry, her fists pummeling the air in front of her.

''Diaper . . . bag . . .'' Darby moaned.

Wishing he'd paid more attention to Darby those few times she'd fed the baby, he peered into the bag, studying the paraphernalia inside. There were diapers and blankets, indecipherable packages and objects, but he ignored them all, reaching for the plastic bottle, a roll of liners, a nipple and cuff. Sporting the items in one hand, he grabbed the can of formula and put them on the dresser top. Quickly reading the labels, he stretched the baglike liner over the top of the hollow bottle, popped open the can of premixed formula, poured it in the liner, and screwed on the nipple top.

''Warm . . .'' he heard Darby say.

Running water from the tap, he waited until it was hot, and then let the water run over the bottle for a bit.

After shaking it, he went back into the main room and scooped the baby into his arms. By this time she was howling, flailing her arms and kicking at the blanket swaddled around her feet.

Christian wasn't exactly sure how he was supposed to get the formula inside the baby. From what he'd seen, there was some rocking and cooing and patting involved. For his purposes, he hoped that sticking the nipple into the kid's mouth would suffice.

As soon as the bottle touched Sissy's lips, she began sucking, her cries of distress melting into peevish snuffles, then grunts of pleasure.

Christian grinned. Sissy stared suspiciously in his direction, but since she was hungry, she was willing to put up with him. At least for a few minutes.

Darby roused only once to say, "Burp..." before she faded into exhaustion again.

Christian took the bottle from the baby's mouth.

She immediately began to cry, but since Darby hadn't roused, he supposed he should follow her instructions.

Draping Sissy over his shoulder, he patted her back as he'd seen Darby do. The baby's squalls eased, becoming more of a series of irritated grunts.

"So are you going to burp, kid, or what?"

The baby didn't respond other than to kick him with feet the size of rubber erasers.

"Come on," he encouraged, wondering what would happen if she didn't burp. Something horrible, most likely. Maybe her stomach would explode.

He patted a little harder. This time, he was rewarded with a deep, throaty belch, one worthy of a veteran drinker at an all-night bar.

Holding her up, Christian looked closely at the infant's face, studying her saucy grin.

"You're pretty proud of yourself, aren't you?"

She waved at him with both fists.

Feeling a little more comfortable with the task he'd been given, Christian settled her into his arm again, and gave her the bottle. As she sucked greedily, he regarded her mother on the bed.

Should he call for some kind of doctor? Take her to an emergency room?

But even as the thought occurred, he shelved it until later. He would wait a few hours and see if bed rest would help. If not, then he'd take matters into his own hands.

The baby was growing still in his arms, the sucking sounds becoming more infrequent. Glancing down, he saw that even though the baby had slept most of the afternoon, she was growing tired yet again.

When she appeared to have stopped eating, he eased the bottle from her lips. There was still more than half of the formula left, but since he hadn't known how much to make, he decided he wouldn't worry about such a detail. At least not as long as the baby was still sleeping.

Setting the baby against his shoulder, he patted her back. After several minutes, he heard a smaller, more ladylike belch.

Tucking the blanket around her body, he stood, ready to put her down for the night, then paused indecisively. There was no crib. Since he would take the other bed, he couldn't put her there. If he set her next to Darby, there was the danger of Darby rolling over in her sleep and hurting the child.

So what?

Studying the small room with its utilitarian furniture, he brightened when he spied the chest of drawers. Retrieving some towels from the bathroom, he laid them in the bottom drawer, then set the baby inside.

Pretty resourceful, Christian.

Yeah, it *was* pretty resourceful.

As well as incredibly atypical.

Turning in a slow circle, he absorbed the cramped motel room, the sleeping child and Darby. When he'd packed his Studebaker for a cross-country vacation, he'd never imagined that he would end up here in Tahoe, sharing a room with a bride and a baby on the lam.

A wry laugh pushed from his throat, but was just as quickly smothered as his eyes fell on Darby.

She hadn't told him the truth. There was more to her escape than merely avoiding publicity. When confronted with a delay in her journey, she'd become fierce. Instinctively Christian sensed that she was worried about Sissy's safety.

But why? She was the baby's mother. No one could change that aspect.

Could they?

Shaking his head at his own suppositions, he took his duffel bag into the bathroom, showered, shaved and changed into a pair of baggy gym shorts and an oversize T-shirt—all the while keeping the door open a crack in order to hear if Darby or the baby needed him.

As he padded to his own bed and slid beneath the sheets, he was forced to admit that it had been a long time since he'd been "needed" by anyone.

Too bad he wouldn't be able to indulge in the sensation for much longer.

Reaching for the phone, he automatically punched out the number of his childhood home. After two rings, he was greeted with a groggy, "Hello."

"Hi, Ma."

"Christian!"

Christian could picture Nan Drake pushing herself into a sitting position and patting the net nightcap she wore over spongy pink curlers.

"Where are you?"

"Tahoe."

"Wonderful. Your father and I went through that area on a road trip when you were young. Do you remember?"

Judging by the home movies he'd been forced to endure throughout his adolescence, he'd been about three at the time.

"No. Not really."

"You had an adorable red cowboy hat and chaps and you wore them every day. You were so sure you'd see Little Joe from 'Bonanza,' you could barely sleep at night."

Christian shifted uncomfortably. His mother's voice was filled with indulgence. His glance shifted to the baby in the drawer and he wondered what it was about children that made most people turn to Jell-O.

"Where will you be heading next?"

Christian jerked his attention back from the infant. "I'm not sure."

"Not sure? You usually have your route planned out days in advance."

"Yeah, well, I've run into a snag."

"Not car trouble." He heard the tension in his mother's voice.

"No. I picked up a temporary passenger."

His mother's panic radiated through the lines. "Christian Alexander Drake. What have I told you about picking up hitchhikers."

His mother's immediate response caused him to laugh. "I haven't picked up a hitchhiker, Mom. I ran into a...lady in distress."

"Oh?" It was clear that she still wasn't reassured. "What kind of lady?"

He knew what was running through her mind. Some woman dressed in stiletto heels, smoking a cigar and calling him her sugar daddy.

"Ma, it's nothing to worry about. I promise. I ran into an old friend." It was a lie, but a harmless one. "She and her baby—"

"Baby!"

"She has a baby girl."

"How old?"

"Little, Ma. Really little. Anyway, my friend had to get to Tahoe, so I offered her a ride." Another stretch of the truth.

"There's something you aren't telling me, Christian."

"Well, I gave her some of the munchies I bought and she . . . well, she got food poisoning."

"Christian Alexander!"

"It wasn't my fault. The expiration date on the juice had expired."

"By how much?"

"A . . . couple of years."

His mother huffed, snickered, then chortled aloud. "You always did have a talent for getting yourself into impossible scrapes." Before he could comment, she said, "I hope you're staying with your friend tonight."

"Yes, Ma. I am."

"You help her with that baby."

"I will—I have."

"And don't you dare leave either one of them on their own until your friend is one-hundred percent better."

"I won't, Ma. I promise."

"What's your number there?"

He pulled the phone to him and recited the numbers listed on the information card.

"Thank you, son. You know I worry about you when you're out in that rattletrap of a car."

Christian fought a grin. His mother thought anything older than a current model Cadillac was a "rattletrap car."

"Call me tomorrow so I know you aren't lying dead on the road somewhere."

"I will, Ma."

"Good boy. You sleep well tonight."

"I will, Ma. Good night."

The receiver clattered into the cradle, but a glance at Darby assured Christian that she hadn't awakened. Sighing, he stacked the pillows under his head, settled into a comfortable position beneath the blankets, allowing his muscles to relax bit by bit. After all that had happened, he was incredibly tired. He'd be able to sleep like a rock until nine or ten. It would feel good to sleep in. So very, very good.

Christian grinned into the darkness, congratulating himself on all he'd accomplished—especially in regards to the baby. Wouldn't his mother be surprised if she could see how well Christian had cared for the infant.

As if on cue, Christian heard a sniffle coming from the dresser drawer. Then a hiccup. A sob.

Waaaa!

Christian's eyes squeezed closed and he fought the urge to swear.

Evidently he wasn't the hotshot baby-sitter he'd thought himself to be.

Chapter Four

Bit by bit Darby was pulled from a cocoon of sleep by the smells of antiseptic, soap and a faint trace of coffee and bacon. Odd. How very odd.

Her lashes fluttered and she focused on a dimly lit room decorated in muted plaids. Two beds. A large, curtain-covered window. A dresser. The sound of a shower running.

In an instant, her whole body stiffened.

You're in a hotel. A hotel!

Immediately she scrambled to pull the covers to her chin, wondering what sort of wild party she'd attended, which had rendered her unconscious in a room she didn't remember, with...*someone* she didn't remember.

No, no, no!

She sat upright, her head pounding. The blankets shifted and she glanced down.

Clothed. She was completely clothed.

Groaning, she cradled her head in her hands, knowing that at any second her skull was going to split and her stomach rebel the effort to contain a wave of nausea.

The squeak of a door alerted her and she ran her fingers through her hair. But as a masculine shape stepped around the divider, she grew even more still.

Christian Drake.

Darby stared at him, absorbing the damp hair, broad, water-dappled shoulders and lean, washboard stomach. Immediately she remembered it all, dashing from the church, getting into this man's car, convincing him to take her to Tahoe, then getting sick, oh, so sick.

He was watching her carefully, obviously unsure how she would react to his presence.

"I forgot my clothes." He gestured to the duffel bag, which lay open on the opposite bed. "I thought you'd still be asleep."

Darby didn't know how she was supposed to respond, so she ignored his lack of clothing as best she could—a nearly impossible feat considering the appearance of the man in front of her.

You didn't notice before that he had a body like that? the little voice inside her mocked.

"Sissy?" she rasped, surprised at how her voice emerged so dry and weak.

He nodded in the direction of the bureau and she noted for the first time that one of the drawers had been removed and lay on the floor. From her vantage point, she was able to see a bundle of blankets and the rounded shape of Sissy's rear poking into the air.

"I need to—"

"I already fed her," Christian inserted before she could finish her statement.

Darby's brows rose. She couldn't help it. "*You* fed her?"

Christian adopted an injured expression even as he crossed to the bed and retrieved his duffel bag. "I've been up all night with the kid."

His tone was disgruntled, but not angry and Darby couldn't prevent the way her jaw dropped.

"*You* took care of her?"

"Yeah. I did. There's no need to act so surprised."

She supposed he was right, but he'd been so uncomfortable in Sissy's presence the day before that it was hard to imagine his caring for her all night long.

"Thanks."

He didn't even acknowledge her comment. Wadding his clothes in his hand, he disappeared in the direction of the bathroom again.

With each step he took, Darby leaned forward to catch the very last sight of him, of his strong back, muscular calves.

An odd breathlessness gripped her lungs, one she recognized as being completely inappropriate for the situation. She was sick, she was tired, she was sharing a room with a total stranger. Now wasn't the time to be going all goo-goo eyed at the sight of his body. His nearly naked body. One streaked with water and tanned to a golden brown...

Stop it!

But even after her mental castigation, Darby couldn't completely tamp down her reaction. Nor could she contain her curiosity about this man. He had been far more helpful to her than most strangers would have been in the same situation. He had liberated her from an ill-fated wedding, given her a ride out of the state, comforted her when she'd been sick, and watched over Sissy through the night. It was amazing, positively amazing. She was so grateful to him and so very, very...

Guilty.

Oh, so guilty.

What right did she have to dump her problems in another person's lap? The man was on vacation, after all, and she had foisted herself into his plans. She should be ashamed of herself. Completely and utterly ashamed.

Thoroughly chastised by her own conscience, she threw back the covers and swung her legs to the ground. But when she tried to stand, a blackness invaded her vision and spots danced before her eyes. Even so, the faintness was nothing compared to the sudden roiling of her stomach.

"What do you think you're doing?"

She heard Christian speaking to her from far away.

"I have to...get going."

"I don't think so."

He touched her shoulder—barely tapped it—and she lost her balance. Sinking onto the bed, she looked up at him accusingly.

"You shouldn't have done that."

"I'll have to disagree with you there. Your skin has gone green again."

She peered around him at the mirror and blanched even more when she caught sight of her own face. Her hair was sticking up at all angles, making the pallor of her skin that much more apparent. Her eyes appeared to have burned dark circles into her skin, and her features were gaunt and strained.

Her stomach lurched again, and she allowed herself to be pushed into the pillows.

"I'll just rest for a minute."

"Uh-huh."

He settled onto his own bed and retrieved the remote control, which had been attached to the nightstand with a plastic spring.

"You don't have to stay here," Darby insisted, ignoring the cold sweat popping out on her upper lip. "I've delayed your vacation long enough."

He didn't answer, even though a muscle flicked in his cheek. Indeed, he seemed to be paying more attention to the television programs that were flashing by at a dizzying speed.

Her stomach lurched and she squeezed her eyes closed saying, "Did you hear me? You can go if you want."

"Uh-huh."

She waited for some kind of farewell speech, but it wasn't forthcoming. When she peered through her lashes, it was to discover that he had made himself quite comfortable and didn't seem inclined to move.

"When will you be leaving?" she prompted, praying even as she did so that he would give her at least an hour's notice. With one more hour's sleep, she was sure that she would be back to her old self.

She noted the way Christian's lips thinned slightly before he answered her question. "I don't know when I'll be going."

Darby peered at him in suspicion, then wilted in defeat.

"You aren't going to take my offer and escape, are you?"

"Nope."

"I can take care of myself, you know," she insisted

"I'm sure you can."

"Sissy will be all right, too. She's still at that age where she sleeps a good deal."

"Maybe during the day."

On that point, she had to agree. Sissy did tend to do most of her playing and fussing during the wee hours of the night.

"Mr. Drake—"

He sighed. "Christian."

"Christian, you really don't have to stick around—spend your day in this cramped hotel room—due to some sort of loyalty you feel you owe me."

He shot her a glance, then looked away. "I don't feel as if I owe you anything."

"Then why? Why are you staying?"

He opened his mouth, paused, then shrugged. "I haven't decided yet. Maybe it's because I'm tired myself and I've been struck by the 'lazies.' Maybe it's because it's been a long time since I've had a clean bed and fresh, dry towels. Maybe it's because I'm dying for room service and some cable television." He reached for the plastic menu on the shelf under the nightstand. "Any way you look at it, though, you're stuck with me."

"Stuck" wasn't exactly the word she would have used. Not at all. Especially when her eyelids were growing incredibly heavy and her stomach was beginning to lose its overt sensitivity.

"Thank you, Christian," she murmured as she felt sleep overtaking her.

From a million miles away, she thought she heard him say, "You're welcome."

CHRISTIAN WAITED until he was sure that Darby was asleep before exhaling. He was so sure that she would question him further about his reasons for lingering. If she did, he would have to admit that he'd been ready to pack his bags and be on his way if it hadn't been for a quick call to his mother.

Damn. He was thirty-four years old. He was a successful entrepreneur and craftsman. He'd lived years in foreign—and oftentimes primitive—situations. But he still couldn't bring himself to disobey his mother. Pitiful. Absolutely pitiful. And because of his maternal subservience, his vacation was being delayed and he was stuck in a hotel room with a deathly ill bride on the run.

And a baby. A *baby,* for hell's sake.

Thank heaven Darby hadn't called his bluff. If she had, she would have discovered that he was no baby whiz. As a matter of fact, he was beginning to believe that kid scared him more than any creature he'd encountered in the Amazon.

He'd fed Sissy, calmed her, soothed her. Then, once he'd managed to get her back to sleep, he'd lain awake, staring at the baby, sure that she'd stopped breathing, that he'd improperly fed her, that her diaper had fallen off. But each time he'd crept to the bureau to check her, she'd been sleeping soundly, her mouth moving in some sort of sucking motion as if she were dreaming of bottles or pacifiers. Reassured, he'd crept back to his bed, only to have her take a deep breath and begin to scream. By dawn, he'd been a nervous wreck.

This morning, feeding her had been less of trial, merely because he'd known what to expect and had a bottle prepared long before she began to cry. But it had been apparent from the baby's reaction that she wasn't used to his care, she didn't like the way she was being held and burped, and she wanted her mother.

Sighing, he eyed the menu more intently. How much longer could food poisoning last? Surely not much more than twenty-four hours. Darby would be able to assume her own responsibilities tomorrow. Then he would be released from the promise he'd given his mother and...

And what? What would he do next?

Growling impatiently at his own thoughts, he picked up the receiver. Breakfast smells had been wafting into their room for hours, probably coming from the direction of the coffee shop. He'd get some food into his stomach. Once he had some fuel for his brain, maybe he wouldn't be feeling like a heel for abandoning the woman before she reached whatever destination she had in mind.

Lifting the receiver, he punched the appropriate number.

"Room Service."

"This is two-eleven. I want the Hungry Man's Breakfast, steak well-done, hash browns, scrambled eggs, orange juice, wheat toast—"

"*Waaaa!*"

Christian's eyes squeezed closed. "And a couple of aspirin."

WHEN DARBY WOKE again, it was to a shadowy room and the crying of a baby.

Her baby.

No, not hers. Not for much longer.

Sitting up in bed, she rubbed her eyes and was relieved to find that her head no longer ached, and her stomach...

It felt fine. Normal. In fact, she was famished.

"Christian?"

At her call, he stepped from the bathroom, holding a squalling baby against his chest. He looked so ill at ease with the situation, she almost smiled. Almost. There was something about the sight of the child cradled against a chest so firm and broad that doused her humor and inspired several completely different emotions. Interest, attraction, allure.

"Are you up to taking her?" he asked without preamble.

She nodded and he set the baby in her arms, surrendering the bottle as well.

Sissy blinked up at Darby with tear-filled eyes, hiccuped, then offered a shuddering sigh.

"There, now, sweetie," Darby crooned. "That's no way to act when a man is giving you his undivided attention."

The infant wasn't interested in her words of wisdom. As soon as the nipple neared her mouth, she began sucking, drinking the milk with greedy, distraught gulps as if this were the last time she would eat for a week.

"I hope she hasn't given you too much trouble," Darby said, glancing up at her rescuer.

Now that she was feeling better, she found his gaze harder to hold. She was abruptly conscious of her sleep-rumpled attire and pillow-hair.

"She wasn't too bad."

His tone was so noncommittal, that Darby knew he'd been about to lose his patience. Evidently she'd awakened just in time.

"I take it she's been cranky."

He snorted and sank into one of the chairs. "I doubt it was her fault. I'm not much good with babies."

Darby wanted to dispute such a statement, but he didn't look as if he was ready to entertain her opinion.

"She doesn't seem any worse for the experience" was all she said.

He shrugged. "I can't say the same for my wardrobe."

Darby resisted the urge to grin. "How many shirts did she spit on?"

"Three."

She gestured toward the diaper bag on the floor. "Didn't you use the burping cloths?"

Judging by his blank expression, he hadn't.

"There's some little flannel cloths with crocheted trim around them."

He dragged the diaper bag close and rooted through the contents, finally retrieving the oblong strips. He studied them as if they were some new alloy he intended to use in one of his bridges. Then he tossed one in her direction.

"I guess I should have thought there was already a solution to the problem."

She hid another smile and centered her attention on the infant.

"I take it you haven't been around many babies."

"They don't usually have the credentials to work on my team."

"What kind of credentials?"

She looked up to find he was studying her intently, his dark eyes slightly narrowed.

Darby shifted self-consciously, supposing she should have run a comb through her hair before taking the baby, but she'd been more concerned about relieving him of the responsibility than her appearance.

"At least a master's degree."

She blinked. "Beg pardon?"

"If a baby's going to work on my crew, she ought to have a masters' degree."

Darby pulled a face at his tongue-in-cheek humor. "I need to reimburse you for all the trouble we've caused you."

"You don't owe me anything," he said dismissingly.

"But I do. I'd like to pay for your gas, this hotel and any other expenses you've incurred on our behalf."

His eyes became steely. "You don't have to do that. I was glad to help."

Darby doubted he'd been all that "glad" but she knew that she would risk offending him if she pressed the point. "Then the hotel bill is mine."

"Don't worry about it."

Sighing, she tried another tack. "At the very least, let me buy you dinner."

Several seconds passed without an answer, but he finally nodded. "Fine. I'll agree to that."

Darby grinned in relief. "Good. I'm starving."

"You've got your color back."

"A color other than green, you mean."

Showing a great deal of gentlemanly restraint, he refrained from commenting.

Darby waited until the baby had been fed and burped, her diaper changed and her clothes exchanged for a fresh set before laying the baby on a spread-out blanket.

"Can you watch her for a minute while I shower?"

Christian had turned on a news program and propped his back against the headboard.

"Sure."

CHRISTIAN WATCHED as Darby gathered the shopping bag that held a change of clothes. He supposed that any other man would have been elated at his current situation. After all, he was marooned in a hotel room with a beautiful woman. Granted, she'd been sick, her hair was a mess, her cheeks pale from her ordeal. But there was no denying her elegance and infinite appeal.

But Christian wasn't any man. The last thing he wanted was to spend any of his vacation time with a woman, elegant or not. He had some serious vacationing to do and only two months to do it. Then, he would be on his way to Thailand for another two-year stint at bridge building.

Picking up the remote, he thanked heaven that Darby was feeling better. By morning, he could be on his way.

The channels flashed by as Christian made his way toward ESPN. One channel shy of the mark, he grimaced when he saw the credits for "The Gossip Exchange." His mother was an aficionado for the show. Why she indulged in the tabloid program, he didn't know.

He was about to punch the channel button when Christian saw a flashing photograph of a bride running from a church. Funny. The woman looked just like.

Darby.

"So where would you like to go?"

Vaguely Christian heard Darby speaking to him from the bathroom, but his eyes were rooted to the screen and his thumb pushed the volume control.

"Christian?"

From the corner of his eye, Christian noted that Darby had emerged from the bathroom. She followed his gaze, glancing at the television, where she found her own picture staring back at her.

"... 'Gossip Exchange' has the exclusive interview with the distraught groom, Chauncey Fitch, who was left at the altar by his bride. Darby Simms, a member of Ricardo Yvonne's design staff, deserted her multimillionaire fiancé to run away with this man—"

There was a fuzzy, close-up still of Christian's face as he looked over his shoulder in the direction of the church.

Christian stiffened.

"—Christian Drake, CEO of Drake Enterprises. According to sources within the company, Drake has been out of the country for over two years."

The camera zoomed into focus on the commentator's face, on the way her eyebrows rose in disbelief. "If this is the case, then how did the two of them meet? Could it be that they've been seeing each other secretly for months as many insiders claim? Or is there a much darker motive behind the whole story? One motivated by greed, lust, perhaps even revenge?"

There was a beat of pointed silence, then, "We'll have more on the story during our next edition. This is Marcia Crawford. Thank you for joining us for this week's 'Gossip Exchange.'"

The show's theme had barely finished when the phone rang. Christian knew instinctively who it would be.

Lifting the receiver to his ear, he said, "Hello, Ma."

"*That's* the woman with food poisoning? That's her?"

He sighed. "Yes."

"Why didn't you tell me?"

"Ma, I—"

"Please tell me the two of you haven't eloped."

"Ma, I told you yesterday—"

"Because if you've married the girl without your family there—"

"Ma, I told you, I helped a lady in distress, nothing more. The two of us aren't involved." He glanced at Darby and added emphatically, "In any way."

His remark was met with a long silence. "There's more to this story than you're telling me."

"I've told you everything I know."

Another beat of quiet.

"Well, you see to it that you don't just run off until you're sure that girl is all right, you hear?"

"Yes, Ma."

"Promise?"

Again, he sighed. Two minutes on the phone with his mother and he was eight years old. "I promise."

After exchanging their goodbyes, he replaced the phone.

"Your mother?" Darby asked hesitantly.

"She's a fan of the show."

Darby groaned. Walking to the set, she punched the Power button.

"I guess it was too much to hope that the media would leave us alone."

"Us? *Us?*"

Darby grimaced. "I meant the baby and me. I swear, I never meant to get you involved in any of this."

"Well, I'm sure as hell involved in it now," he exclaimed, wondering who else had seen the show. His sister? His colleagues? They'd never let him hear the end of this. Christian Drake, confirmed bachelor, the Iron Man, caught running off with some unknown woman.

Darby stood in front of him, wringing her hands, looking chagrined and very uncertain. "Let me take you to dinner. I'll explain everything." Muttering to herself, she added, "But I'd rather not do it on an empty stomach."

Chapter Five

In the end, it was Darby who chose the restaurant. As far as she could tell, Christian wasn't speaking to her—not that she could blame him. He'd come to her aid like a knight in shining Studebaker, and she'd repaid him by involving him in her own personal dilemmas. It didn't matter that she'd never planned for such a thing to happen. The die was already cast and it was up to her to set things right.

She chose a quiet little place perched above the lake. The restaurant reeked of atmosphere and muted gentility—facts she hoped would work on her behalf. Maybe after they'd both had something to eat, relaxed over some coffee, chatted about trivial matters, she would be in a position to help Christian understand what she was doing with a baby and a mothball-scented wedding dress.

"Dining room or terrace?" the maître d' asked as they stepped into a vaulted foyer reminiscent of the Ponderosa with its log walls and timbered beams.

"Terrace, I think," Darby replied before Christian could respond. The fresh air would do him good.

As it was, he was looking pinched and strained around the mouth.

The maître d' glanced at the baby carrier she held, then at their jeans and T-shirts. It was obvious he didn't approve—either of the child or the casual mode of dress she and Christian had adopted—but at least he had a flair for discretion and kept his thoughts to himself.

"This way, please."

The man took two oversize menus from a stack at his podium and led them through the maze of dimly lit tables adorned with the finest in crystal and flatware. By the time they'd gone halfway, even Darby was feeling self-conscious about their attire. Especially when the whispers began, the muted murmurs, the starts of recognition.

Blast it all, evidently she and Christian hadn't been the only ones to witness the galling gossip program.

"They're staring at us."

The low comment came from behind.

"It's your imagination," she insisted under her breath.

"I don't think so."

Thankfully they were given a table in the far corner of the terrace, one screened from view by a low rock wall and a trellis filled with ivy. Somehow, Darby sensed that the position was due more to the maître d's snobbishness than his concern over their privacy, but she wasn't about to quibble.

She settled the baby carrier onto an empty chair, then noted that Christian had moved behind her own place and was waiting. Evidently, she thought as she sank into the plush seat, chivalry was not completely dead. She intended to take that as a good sign.

"Sergei will be your waiter. Would you like to speak to the sommelier?"

Darby had already begun to examine her menu and peeked over the top at Christian. "Wine?"

He shook his head. "I want a beer, anything domestic, in the bottle, don't bother bringing a glass, but make sure the beer's well chilled."

The maître d' was not able to completely hide his disdain at Christian's choice of beverages.

"And you, madam? Will you be having wine?"

Darby seriously considered the choice—right now she could use a bit of wine—but she decided against it. At least until her confessions were finished and she no longer needed all her wits about her.

"Nooo," she drawled with infinite regret. "I'll have a lime and soda instead, heavy on the lime."

"Yes, madam."

The man backed away with obvious relief, leaving Darby alone with Christian—well, with Christian and Sissy. But since the baby had been fed and bathed, she was sure the infant was out for the count for at least a couple of hours. There would be no diversion coming from her end of the table.

"Order whatever you'd like," Darby said, her mouth watering from the choices being offered. Her stomach growled in a most unladylike manner.

Christian's eyes creased in amusement and his lips twitched, but he didn't allow himself a real smile. She sensed she would be on the giving end of his most somber expression until he felt he'd been given the answers he deserved.

"Good evening," a low, Slavic-tinged voice melted into the darkness. "I'm Sergei, your waiter."

Darby glanced up to see a Chippendales-like waiter bowing in a courtly manner.

"Have you had time to look over the menu."

"Mmm." She tore her eyes away from the overtly handsome man to find Christian glaring at her. "I think I'm ready to order."

"Very good."

She pointed to the appropriate spot on the heavy parchment. "I would like the stuffed mushrooms as an appetizer, but I want them without the braised butter, or not at all."

The waiter nodded, and Darby heartily wished he had some sort of paper to record her order. It always made her nervous when an eating establishment prided themselves on the powers of their memory. She had very particular tastes and she wanted things prepared right the first time.

"I'd also like a Caesar salad, no croutons, dressing on the side. Then I'd like a potato, baked, with a dollop of yogurt rather than sour cream, but no butter, a portion of the sweet potato casserole mentioned with the orange and pecan pork chops—but I don't want the chops. I want the steamed vegetables and extra bread instead."

Poor Sergei's eyes grew wider with each request and it was evident that he was questioning his own ability to remember everything. "Very good, madam," he murmured as he reached for the menu.

"No, leave it here. I'd like to study the dessert descriptions."

"Of course. And you, sir?" Sergei asked, clearly worried that Christian was going to be as difficult with his selections.

"I'll have the salad with all the dressing you want, the sirloin steak—burn it—and you can put her butter and sour cream on my potato."

Sergei beamed at Christian as if he'd seen the promised land.

"Wonderful, wonderful!" he exclaimed, taking Christian's menu and backing toward the shallow stone steps that led into the main portion of the restaurant.

"You really should watch your fat content," Darby said for lack of a better thing to say. Then she wished she could have retrieved the comment. She didn't want to antagonize the man before they'd even started.

"I've had a diet of tropical fruit and fish for the better part of two years. I don't care what this does to my cholesterol count."

Well, he told you.

"You're a vegetarian, huh."

Christian's remark wasn't a question.

"Mostly."

His brows rose.

"I like what I like."

"Ahhh."

Sergei returned with her mushrooms and she put the plate between them. "Help yourself."

"No, thanks. You asked them to hold the taste, so I'll wait for something that's bad for me."

Pulling a face at him, she speared one of the mushrooms, chewed, then sighed when the delicately spiced food filled her tongue.

"This is good—really good."

Since he'd already refused her offer, she didn't bother to ask again, but began to take the edge off her hunger.

"Explain what's going on, Darby."

Her enthusiasm for the food died in an instant and it became difficult to swallow.

"I thought we'd eat first."

"I want to know now."

"You'll be leaving us soon," she countered, still hesitating.

"I still want to know exactly what's going on here."

Chewing the last of her mushroom, she washed it down with a gulp of cool ice water from the goblet by her plate. Sergei chose that moment to bring their drinks and she caught his arm. "I've changed my mind about the wine. Bring me a glass of your best white."

"Yes, madam."

Christian took a sip of his beer from the bottle and waited.

"It's a long story."

"I've got time."

She glanced down at the baby, but Sissy lay with her cheek pressed into the softness of her blankets.

"The baby isn't really mine."

She didn't think that she could shake Christian's stern air, but she was wrong. He swore under his breath and glanced over both shoulders before stabbing an accusing finger into the air.

"I told you I didn't want to be involved in anything illegal."

"No, no." She hurriedly interrupted. "It isn't anything like that. I have official guardianship."

His body relaxed, inch by subtle inch, the chocolate color of his eyes warming again. "So this isn't some elaborate kidnapping scheme?"

"No."

"Or a desperate custody battle?"

"No. In fact, it's the opposite."

His brow furrowed, but the waiter chose that moment to return with her wine, giving her a few minutes to collect her thoughts.

"I suppose this whole situation began several years ago, when I was given a special-needs scholarship to a girl's academy in New England."

"Special needs?"

"My parents had died and there was little money for the necessities, let alone an exclusive finishing school." She ran her fingers up and down the stem of her glass, absorbing the cool, smooth texture as if it were some sort of talisman. "While I was there, I met and became friends with Eloise Nashton."

She waited for him to offer some sort of response, but when he remained silent, she supposed the name would not be familiar to a man who would have little interest in the society page.

"She was the heir to the Nashton China Works, a million-dollar corporation that has been in business since the eighteenth century."

"Old money," he murmured.

"Very old and very prestigious." She took another sip of the wine, then continued. "Anyhow, Eloise and I became fast friends—I doubt we ever spent any real time apart. I roomed with her, studied with her, even spent my vacations with her family. When her father died after a long illness, I consoled her. When she wasn't accepted into a Parisian art school, I encouraged her to study here in the United States."

She sighed. "Then, when it came time for college, we were separated. I attended the Sorbonne and she . . . well, Eloise wasn't that fond of school. It had always been a struggle for her. So after two semesters, she gave up and became embroiled in the jet-setting life."

This was where the story grew hard to tell and she was grateful for the dim lighting. "I was disturbed with how she altered over the next few years. She became less interested in her painting and was consumed with the who's who of the society crowd. I think her father's death had a lot to do with her transformation. She found herself very alone and burdened with company decisions—something she had no training for whatsoever."

Again, she drank the wine, this time draining half of what remained. "A few months ago, I obtained a position working with a New York designer and Eloise came to see me there. She was positively radiant . . . as well as very pregnant. To say I was shocked would put it mildly. I'd had no indication whatsoever. Never once had she mentioned a 'special someone' or that she was contemplating motherhood. We shopped, we talked, we laughed . . .''

Her throat grew tight. "I know now I should have paid more attention. I should have asked more questions. But I didn't want to pry into her personal affairs."

A lump had wedged behind her larynx and she knew she needed to say her piece as quickly as possible.

"Six weeks later, I received a telegram informing me that Sissy had been born. Two weeks after that, Eloise's housekeeper showed up on my doorstep, carrying the baby, and bringing the news that Eloise had died when an avalanche in Switzerland pushed her car off the road."

She pushed her glass away rather than draining the contents as she wanted to do. "I discovered later that Sissy was to be my ward until she could be reunited with her father."

"Who is . . .'' Christian prompted.

Darby's shoulders lifted. "I don't know."

His mouth dropped ever so slightly. "You don't know?"

"No. Eloise's instructions were incomplete—which if you knew her, was not an unusual occurrence. She was always moving from one project to another, one thought to another. She rarely wrote anything down, and automatically assumed that people knew exactly what she meant." Her lips pursed. "Added to that was the fact that Eloise considered herself immortal.

I wouldn't be surprised if the portion of the will that outlined my guardianship was drafted while she was still on painkillers due to some minor corrective surgery, which had been done at the same time. She probably wasn't even aware of the seriousness of her request.''

The attempt at levity had the desired effect, lessening some of the tension.

"So how does all this lead up to the Wedding Forum and a runaway bride?''

''I was given Eloise's diary as part of her personal effects. I spent the better part of a week poring over the pages and amassing clues.'' She grimaced. "Unfortunately Eloise was always very discreet when committing things to writing, so I was only able to narrow the candidates down to six men.''

"One of them being Chauncey Fitch.''

"I realize now, I was incredibly naive. I hopped a plane, knocked on his door with a baby in my arms and bluntly asked him if Eloise Nashton had been his lover and Sharece was his daughter.'' Her bark of laughter was bitter. "Now, I see that it was the money that convinced him to lie and claim Sissy as his own.''

"How did you know she wasn't?''

"His aunt confessed to me that he was sterile. A bout with the mumps caused that little condition,'' she added tartly.

She caught Christian's quick grin.

"So you hightailed it out of the church.''

"You bet I did. He'd suggested a marriage of convenience so that I could continue as Sissy's mother.

But I wasn't about to trap myself to a low-down, sneaky, lying, thief.''

His grin intensified, causing her stomach to tingle in an odd, enervating way.

"So you hijacked me and came to Tahoe?"

"I wanted to avoid as much publicity as possible." On impulse, she bent forward and touched his hand. The contact was electric, sending a jolt of awareness through her fingertips and adding a fervent huskiness to her voice. "I didn't mean to drag you into all this. I swear."

He was looking at their hands, hers pale and small, his large and tanned. Darby had always been attracted to a man's hands. She liked them long and slim and expressive—just as Christian's were. But she had never considered the calluses that could linger on the palms. She found that she liked that fact even more. It proved that he worked hard.

"I'm especially sorry about that gossip show."

He didn't respond in the way she'd expected. Instead he brushed her apology aside and asked, "So what will you do now, Darby?"

She shifted uncomfortably. "I have five other men to investigate. The nearest one is in Utah. Tomorrow, I'll see about getting a plane to Salt Lake City."

Christian met her gaze, his own eyes so dark and fathomless, she found it difficult to look away.

"You're sure that's a good idea?"

She nodded. "I have to find Sissy's father. It's the right thing to do."

"Even if it means giving her up yourself."

She straightened, withdrawing her hand, realizing that this man saw too much. Far too much.

"It's the right thing to do," she repeated.

"How are you going to prevent another man from claiming to be her father?"

Her shoulders grew straight and proud. "I'm not nearly so trusting now."

"Uh-huh." His voice rang with obvious doubt.

"It's true. I know what questions to ask and how to ask them without giving too much information away. And this time," she added firmly, "I'll insist on a DNA test before transferring guardianship."

The waiter arrived with their plates, setting them on the table with all the care of a jeweler displaying his wares. As he did so, Darby took a deep, steeling breath. Her hunger had faded, and in its place was an ever-growing worry. Not for the first time, she found herself wondering, *Am I doing the right thing?* But superseded over that concern was another more insistent worry.

When I do find Sissy's father, how will I ever give her up?

SISSY WAS GROWING FUSSY as they returned to the hotel room, and Darby was glad for the diversion. The baby's cries helped to drown out her own misgivings about the situation. Now that she was well, was she supposed to arrange for her own room? Or would such a suggestion insult her unwilling host and make him think that she didn't trust him?

Deciding that if a change was going to be made, Christian would have to be the first to suggest it, she made her way inside and began measuring formula. When she returned to the main room, Christian had settled on the bed with his back to the headboard, his legs stretched out and crossed at the ankle.

"So you're going to fly to Salt Lake, huh?" he asked as she sank into the chair and began to feed the baby.

Sissy was resistant at first, turning her head away from the nipple.

"Yes. It's less than an hour, I'm sure."

"What will you do once you're there?"

"I told you. I'm going to track down the next father."

"How will you approach him?"

When she didn't answer, he gave her an arch look, his eyes glinting with far more humor than they had a right to do.

"Come on. You can practice with me."

Sensing the challenge lacing his tone, she said, "I think I'll approach him and say, "Hello, Nick Rassmussen, I have a big surprise for you, but only if you have a healthy bank account yourself."

"Subtle."

"I thought so."

Sissy uttered a plaintive cry, pushing at the bottle.

"So what are you going to say, Darby? Really."

She jiggled the baby, wondering why Sissy was so fretful. "I don't know," she admitted after a minute. "I suppose I'll have to wing it."

He thought for a minute, then said, "May I make a suggestion?"

"Sure."

"Why don't you invite him to dinner, or for drinks, under the guise of being a reporter? That way you could ask him lots of questions without appearing too suspicious. You could say you're from a European paper and you're doing an in-depth story on Eloise's life."

Darby's brows rose. "That's a great idea, Christian. Thank you."

Christian. The name hung in the room, sounding much too familiar. But how could that be? They'd shared a room together, her illness, the responsibilities of a child?

"So where will *you* be going next, Christian?"

"I don't know,"

His answer was flip, but she noticed that the map on the bed was open to the state of Utah.

"How long are you planning to travel the country?"

"At least six weeks."

"You don't have an itinerary?"

"No. I'm going to do my best to wander around the country until it's time to report for my next job."

"Where will you be going next?"

"Thailand."

Thailand. That was a long way from New York no matter how a person looked at it.

Christian leaned back, layering his hands behind his head and causing his shirt to pull taut over his chest and upper arms. Darby did her best to look away, but time and time again, she found herself gazing at him, studying the crisp waves of his hair, the deep brown of his eyes.

He was a handsome man—in a craggy, rugged sort of way. She had no problem envisioning him swinging from the top of a bridge or walking a beam hundreds of feet off the ground. His whole body seemed to radiate a devil-may-care attitude that should have been off-putting.

But he isn't off-putting.

He's very intriguing.

Very fascinating.

"You like danger, don't you, Christian?"

One of his brows lifted. "Maybe. Maybe that explains why I'm with you."

The words were meant to emerge in a teasing fashion, she knew. But something happened to the phrase midway out of his mouth. His tone became silky, knowing.

Erotic, her little voice added and she squelched it immediately.

Darby instinctively knew she shouldn't respond, but she couldn't help baiting him. "Is that what you think, Christian? That I'm dangerous?"

The last of the humor died from his eyes, being replaced by something much hotter and steelier.

"Yes. I think you're trouble. Especially to a man like me."

"What sort of man is that?"

"A loner. A man who tends to follow his instincts rather than the dictates of society."

"Is that a bad thing?"

"Some people think it is." The chocolaty color of his eyes burned into her skin, making her conscious of the way he scrutinized every inch of her body from top to toe. "You're a very beautiful woman."

The words alone caused a shiver to race up her spine.

"It's been a long time since I've spent any time in the company of anyone like you."

His admission came so grudgingly that Darby's blood pounded with sudden awareness. The room shrunk, becoming a tiny, airless cubicle. Even Sissy's fretfulness didn't break the anticipation that shimmered around them.

"Moreover, I made a promise," he continued.

"A promise?" she echoed weakly. "To whom?"

"My mother."

Vaguely she remembered the phone conversation she'd overheard.

"She made me swear I wouldn't leave you to fend for yourself until you were completely well again."

"Oh."

"Are you completely well?"

Darby's throat grew tight. If she answered yes, he would leave her. Tonight. If she said no, he would stay. Unwillingly.

Christian shifted, breaking the electric silence. "I don't think you should go on the plane tomorrow."

Christian's statement came so suddenly, so bluntly, that she blinked.

"Beg pardon?"

"You're looking quite pale tonight, despite the fact that you've eaten. I think it would be best if we stuck together for another day. Just to make sure. By driving, you'll have time to make plans."

It will give you more time with Sissy.

He didn't say the words aloud, but she knew he was thinking them, just as she was—and that thought alone was enough to make her consider the idea.

It will also give you more time with Christian Drake, her little voice added as much as she tried to squelch it. *You want that, don't you? You want to find out what makes this man tick. You want to find out why he disturbs you so completely.*

"I don't know if it would be...appropriate for me to—"

"Who the hell cares what is appropriate or not?" he demanded lowly, interrupting her. "Nothing about this situation has been 'appropriate,' so why start worrying about appearances now? Come with me to Utah, no strings attached. Once I'm sure you're well, I'll be on my way."

"Why would you even extend such an offer? It's obvious that the baby makes you uncomfortable while I . . ." Her words trailed away.

"While you what?" he urged.

She considered her words carefully and chose the more prudent path. "While I have been more trouble than you imagined, I'm sure."

"As you said, I'm willing to take risks."

"But to what end?"

He thought for some time, then said, "I don't know. I don't know why I want you to come with me. I only know that my instincts are telling me that I should keep you around a while longer."

"Even if it means that the media scrutinizes your every move?"

"I don't give a damn about the media."

"I do," she insisted.

"Why?"

"Because I want the next daddy candidate to be taken by surprise so that his reactions to Sissy will be genuine, not rehearsed."

"I think you worry too much. We've managed to outsmart the media. They have no idea where either of us has gone."

Darby glanced down at Sissy, knowing that she should refuse this man's offer. Until this baby had dropped into her life, she'd always been a person to follow rules and maintain a strict sense of decorum—probably because of her years at a finishing school.

But tonight, she was tempted, so very tempted, to throw caution to the wind.

"The baby *is* a bit fretful," she said slowly.

"The plane would only upset her more."

"Especially if she's coming down with something."

"The car tends to help her sleep."

Darby bit her lip, still wavering. "I'd need more clothes."

"I'm sure we could find a place on our way out of town."

The silence became a living thing, waiting as tensely for her answer as the man on the bed. Through it all, Darby tried to remember why she should be cautious, but she couldn't seem to think. Not while Christian was eyeing her so intently.

But even as she opened her mouth to refuse, her inner voice whispered, *Don't say no. If you do, you'll be sorry for the rest of your life.*

And at that moment, she knew her inner voice was right. If she didn't take a chance with this man, her worst regret in life would come from leaving this man too soon.

"All right," she finally whispered. "I'll go with you."

Chapter Six

They left early the next morning, making a quick stop at a department store so that Darby could renew her supply of formula and diapers, then another dash into a trendy boutique so that she could augment her own wardrobe.

"Don't take too long," Christian warned as Darby slammed the passenger door shut.

"I won't."

He gazed at her in disbelief. How many times had he been left to wait in the car, while his former wife dodged into some store with the promise of, "I'll just be a minute"? He'd learned to expect Rachael to take at least an hour. Or two. Then, when she'd returned, she always chided him for his impatience, putting on a wounded maiden routine because his jobs out of the country prevented her from purchasing the items she needed.

Christian grimaced. She'd been the only engineer's wife in Borneo with a closetful of evening gowns, high-heel shoes and fur wraps.

"I *will* hurry," Darby insisted, bringing his attention back from a past he would rather not remember.

"As much as a woman can, I suppose."

She propped her hands on her hips. "What's that remark supposed to mean?"

"Merely that women and shopping are a dangerous combination."

She huffed in indignation. "Don't you think you're overgeneralizing?"

"Not in my experience."

"And what *is* your experience?"

"My wife was a champion shopper."

Christian wasn't sure, but he thought some of the color bled from her cheeks.

"Wife?"

"My ex-wife."

The explanation seemed to relieve her.

"Thank goodness," she breathed. "I thought I was going to have to explain that gossip segment to your wife as well."

"Not a chance. She's moved on to bigger and better things."

Darby's brows rose. "Such as?"

"A bigger bank account and a husband with a better job."

He knew Darby was about to ask more so he glanced at his watch. She took the none-too-subtle hint and rushed into the shop. Christian was then left with a somber baby who had been kept in her car seat too long.

Glancing back at her, Christian sighed. Sissy offered him a pitiful expression, her lip quivering and her eyes filling with tears. Try as he might, he couldn't resist reaching out to jiggle her seat. It didn't really matter that the baby's mood had not improved since the previous night. It didn't matter that Christian had spent most of the evening with a pillow wrapped around his ears, trying to sleep. Sissy had the darkest, prettiest eyes he'd ever seen, and with one look, Christian could hear his mother's voice echoing in his head.

You take care of her, you hear? I raised you with manners, so you make sure you use them.

"You kept me up all night, kid."

A tear slipped down her cheek.

"Damn," he murmured, jiggling her again. He shouldn't blame the baby for his frustration. His trip hadn't really been delayed all that much, and after vegetating in the hotel room for a day, he hadn't needed the sleep. Add to those reasons the breakfast he'd had—three cups of coffee, a rasher of bacon, three eggs, hashbrowns and enough toast to feed a regiment—he had no reason at all to complain.

Unfortunately Darby's own coffee and dry English muffin hadn't managed to chase away her short temper, he thought as a pair of elderly women stopped to coo at the baby. If anything, the meal had made her more frustrated. In Christian's opinion, her mood was due to the food she ate. His ex-wife had also been fanatical about fat grams and carbohydrates, to the extent that her body had become emaciated and her personality waspish.

"Let's go."

Christian glanced up in surprise as Darby threw her packages into the back. She must have broken a land-speed record in shopping.

"You're done?"

"Yes."

Christian was sure that this was some kind of trick, that she would insist on at least one more stop. But Darby climbed into the car and tossed a smile in the direction of the old women.

The ladies beamed at her.

"Is this your little girl?" one of them asked.

"Mmm," Darby said noncommittally.

"Such a sweet thing," the other one murmured. Then, her gray brows furrowed. "Have we met before?"

Darby glanced at them both and shook her head. "I don't think so." She fastened her seat belt, and Christian immediately started the engine.

The first woman gasped. "I know you! You're the one on the news!"

Her companion scrambled for the video camera.

Christian didn't wait for Darby to reply, but pulled away from the curb and into traffic with the slightest squeal of rubber.

"What's the rush?" Darby demanded, glancing behind her at the two openmouthed women who followed their progress.

"I didn't want to hear what they had to say." He shot her a sidelong glance when she continued to gape at him. "Didn't you notice the establishment next to the boutique?"

Twisting in her seat, she squinted against the wind, then groaned. On the north corner, the Chapel of Eternal Love was nestled in a bunch of trees.

Darby scrunched into her seat. "Those two couldn't possibly have thought we were...that I was..."

But it was clear that Christian believed the worst.

"Anyway," she added. "What does it matter?"

Christian gripped the wheel more tightly. "It doesn't matter."

But it did. Especially if his mother caught wind of the next wrinkle in this escapade.

"I NEED TO TALK TO RICARDO."

Darby plugged one ear with her finger and held the receiver to the other. After several hours spent in polite silence, she and Christian had stopped at a gas station where the proprietor was fond of playing a local country and western station as loud as possible.

"What?"

She could barely hear the voice on the other line. "Ricardo. Ricardo!"

"He isn't here."

Darby's brows rose. "Where is he?"

"He and Debbie went to lunch."

But Ricardo never went to lunch. Not during the designing of a show. Not unless he intended to seduce the woman.

"Damn," she whispered under her breath. When Ricardo started fraternizing with the staff, he forgot about schedules and deadlines, and a majority of the work fell upon his assistant.

An assistant who was thousands of miles away, traveling cross-country with a stranger.

"What time will you be in, Darby? Ricardo said your wedding was called off and you'd be flying straight to New York."

Darby squeezed her eyes shut in frustration. "No. No, I won't be there for at least another week."

"But there's no one in the shop to supervise things."

"Listen, you've got to tell Ricardo that I'm in Utah."

"Utah? I thought you were in San Francisco."

The phone crackled with static and Darby feared she was about to lose the connection. "Tell Ricardo I'll call him tomorrow at ten. Make sure he's there."

"I'll try. But you know how he is when he's hot on the trail of a woman."

As she replaced the receiver, Darby bit her lip. She did know. He would spend every hour of the day in pursuit, abandon his work, then get in a panic about the show. If Darby wasn't there to handle things, he would hire another assistant on the spot. She'd seen the scenario before. In fact, that's how Darby had received her own promotion.

"Trouble?"

She jumped when Christian spoke from a spot behind her shoulder. Whirling, she found him standing a few feet away, bouncing a fractious baby Sissy.

"Yes. My boss was expecting me back right away."

"What are you going to do?"

She thought for a few seconds, then lifted her hands in a helpless gesture. "What can I do? Sissy needs to be delivered to her father. I can't go back to work until I've made an effort to see to the arrangements.''

Moving to his side, she took the baby from Christian's arms. "I'll try to call him again tomorrow. It's the best I can do.'' She did her best to adopt a carefree expression. "Meanwhile, we've only got a few more hours of driving.''

But upon arriving in Park City and settling into her hotel room, Darby turned on the television in time to see an amateur video of Christian, the baby and her tearing away from the curb. As soon as they were out of sight, the camera zoomed in on the chapel's sign.

"Damn,'' she whispered under her breath. "Why are they making such a fuss over us, Sissy? Why should they care what we do and where we go?''

"I see you caught the last few minutes of 'The Gossip Exchange,' '' Christian commented moments later when he pushed open the door she'd left ajar and leaned his shoulder against the jamb.

"I can't believe it,'' she said, shaking her head. "The whole situation is insane. I'm a big Nobody in the celebrity circuit. Why are they blowing this situation out of proportion?''

"I suppose they find the situation titillating.''

"Well, if they don't stop it, the daddy candidates are going to know I'm on my way.''

"So what? Even if they know you're coming, they can't falsify a DNA test.''

Darby stared at him, then grinned. Why hadn't she considered such a possibility herself?

"Besides. Other than my mother and a very limited audience of cable subscribers, not many people watch that show."

"I suppose," she offered grudgingly, but her mood was definitely improving.

Christian straightened.

"How's your stomach feeling?"

Darby hesitated only a fraction of an instant, knowing that she had to tell the truth, but also knowing that this man would leave her as soon as she was completely well.

"It's fine."

"Hungry?"

"Starved."

"Then let's get something to eat."

If the truth were known, Darby was exhausted. The three of them had been traveling nonstop since Tahoe—most of the time spent in a quiet, nerve-racking silence. Right now, Darby wanted nothing more than a long, hot bath, and a good night's sleep. But the thought of having Christian leave without one last outing in his company kept her from refusing.

But even as she reached for the baby carrier, she hesitated. "Maybe we should order room service," she suggested.

His gaze was all-knowing. "You can't hide from every schmuck with a video camera, or every maître d' with a bad attitude toward babies."

"No, but it might be wise to be more discreet in a town where I will be interviewing one of the prospective fathers."

He sighed, planting his hands on his hips, and it was obvious that after being cooped up in a car for hours on end, he didn't relish exchanging such a prison for a hotel room.

"Wait a minute," he ordered, moving back across the hall to his own room.

Darby was half wishing he would keep convincing her to leave the hotel. She hadn't been able to absorb the quaint charm of the resort city as they'd searched for a hotel. She'd been too busy wondering if Christian would suggest sharing a room again—something she knew she shouldn't do. Not when she was healthy again. Not when the hours in the Studebaker had intensified her awareness of him, of his unconscious good looks, his athlete's body and those broad, slender hands gripping the wheel. Luckily Christian must have read her thoughts because he'd suggested that they try to get "rooms" close enough together to coordinate their activities.

The door swung open across the corridor and Christian emerged, a pair of dark glasses and a baseball hat dangling from his fingers.

"Wear these. No one will recognize you."

Darby doubted such a ploy would work, but she didn't argue. Not when she was just as eager to explore their surroundings.

As soon as the baby had been changed and dressed again, they were on their way. Christian drove the Studebaker to the main area of town, a narrow historically registered street that stretched up the mountainside. Either side of the narrow lane was lined with narrow buildings and elaborate, nineteenth-century storefronts.

Darby itched to investigate the interesting shops and boutiques, but she agreed with Christian that the first order of business was food. Dodging into an establishment called the Jumping Frog, they took a booth near the back of the narrow aisle, which led to an outer eating area. Sliding into the darkly paneled cubicle hung with vintage memorabilia, they pored over menus filled with, of all things, Mexican cuisine.

Throwing good nutrition to the four winds, Darby forgot about fat grams and empty calories and ordered exactly what her stomach craved, quesadillas as an appetizer, chips and salsa, a salad drenched in a house vinaigrette dressing and a combination platter that would allow her a sampling of a half-dozen specialties.

"You're obviously feeling better," Christian remarked after she'd ordered.

"Yes, and after treading lightly with my stomach, I'm in the mood for something hot and spicy."

As she uttered the statement, she glanced at him. Their eyes locked.

"Hot and spicy, hmm?" he murmured before looking away, this time at the baby.

Sissy was sleeping, but it was obvious from the pucker between her small brows that she was still irritable.

"Is she sick?"

Darby sipped on the margarita she'd ordered. "I think she's caught a slight cold."

Christian watched the baby as she stirred for a moment, then settled into a deeper sleep. After several minutes, he asked, "So when do you intend to confront Rassmussen?"

"I don't know. Soon, I guess." Darby's voice didn't emerge nearly as strong as she'd wanted. "I think I'll use your idea about masquerading as a reporter. I'll even wear a disguise..." Her words trailed away and she unconsciously looked over Christian's shoulder to the phone booth situated by the front door.

Seeing her gaze, Christian touched her hand to distract her attention. Then, rather than immediately withdrawing, he said, "Don't think about it. Not right now. Enjoy your meal. We can see if he's listed in the directory when we leave."

We. Did he know how that unconscious word gave her comfort? Strength? Had he used it purposely? Or had it been an unconscious slip.

"Agreed?" he asked when she didn't respond.

"Yes. Agreed."

THE MEAL WAS FANTASTIC, freshly prepared and bursting with flavor. Within the first few bites, Christian noted that even Darby's nerves couldn't prevent her from enjoying the fare. When she had finished, she pushed the plate toward Christian.

"Here."

He'd eaten his own food fairly quickly, and couldn't deny that he wouldn't mind trying some of the more exotic treats she'd ordered with her sampler.

"You're sure you don't mind?"

She shook her head, placing a hand on her stomach. "I couldn't eat another bite."

Scooping up a bite of marinated chicken, he nodded in enjoyment. "It's good. Really good."

"I suppose in your travels, you've been exposed to some great food."

He grimaced. "Yes and no. A lot of the time I do my own cooking, so it doesn't really matter if the ingredients are mysterious and new, I'm still a lousy cook." He chewed again, ignoring the fact that there was an intimacy to eating from her dish.

"What was the best meal you had?"

He thought for a minute. "I was in Mexico working on the peninsula, and the woman we hired to help around camp fixed us this great Chinese meal."

"Chinese?"

"Her mother was Korean, her father Scottish and her husband Portuguese, so go figure." He arched a brow. "How about you?"

"My mother's Thanksgiving turkey."

The simple answer tugged at his heart, despite the fact that he didn't want it to. He didn't want to feel anything for this woman. They were destined to part. Probably tonight.

He saw the way Darby looked toward the phone booth, and knew the comment about her mother had reminded her of Sissy's situation.

"Do you want to hit some of the shops before we head back to the hotel?" he asked.

"Mmm-hmm," she responded absently, wiping her hands down the legs of her jeans in an effort to remove the clamminess settling onto her palms. Then she took a deep breath. "Will you watch Sissy?"

Christian nodded, setting the fork down and eyeing Darby intensely as she made her way to the English-style phone booth in the corner.

Sissy offered a garbled cry. Even in her sleep, she'd unconsciously known that Darby had left. Absently Christian wondered if infants had an acute sense of smell that allowed them to tell if their mothers were near. Hadn't he read that information somewhere?

Sissy wriggled and fussed, her face screwing into a cross scowl.

Christian looked to see if Darby would return, but she was already ensconced in the booth.

Reaching out his foot, he jiggled the carrier.

The baby sobbed.

"Come on, Sissy," he coaxed. "Darby will be right back."

The baby took a deep breath and screamed.

Knowing she wouldn't stop if he ignored her, Christian scooped the baby into his arms. To his utter amazement, the baby snuffled, rubbed her face against his shirt, then fell fast asleep.

"I'll be damned," Christian muttered to himself holding her a little more snugly.

THE DIRECTORY for the Park City vicinity was surprisingly small, in Darby's opinion. Even so, she nearly dropped it as she fumbled through the white pages. No Nick Rassmussen. Thumbing to the yellow pages, she looked up Rassmussen Development, and fished a quarter from her pocket.

"Rassmussen Development. How may I direct you?"

"Nick Rassmussen, please."

"Who's calling?"

Darby bit her lip, hesitated, then said, "Inform him that I wish to speak to him concerning Eloise Nashton."

She was put on hold. A long, interminable hold filled with too-loud classical music—some sort of violin concerto that grated on her nerves.

Finally, a deep voice answered, "Yeah."

"Nick Rassmussen?"

"No, this is his brother Roger."

Damn.

"I needed to speak with Nick, please. Is he available?"

There was a long pause, then, "That isn't possible."

Darby's stomach clenched. "May I ask why?"

"Sure, as long as you tell me who you are and why you're calling."

Again, Darby hesitated, then said, "I'm a reporter with the—"

"Reporter, hell. Look, if you're some kind of investigator for the insurance company, you can forget it. Nick is out of the country. He had nothing to do with her accident. He wasn't even in Switzerland at the time. He didn't take her to that resort, and he didn't encourage her to drive through the avalanche warning zone."

"That's not why I need to speak to him."

"Oh." It was clear the man was taken aback. Since Darby had his undivided attention, she decided to use at least a portion of the truth.

"Actually we're doing a story on her infant daughter."

"So why do you want to talk to Nick?"

"There's been some question as to the baby's...paternity, and—"

"And you think *Nick* might be involved?" Rather than becoming upset, the man offered a bark of laughter. "Lady, you've got the wrong guy."

"I merely wanted to talk to him and—"

"Why?" The humor in Roger Rassmussen's voice grew more apparent. "He's got nothing to do with the kid, I can assure you. Nick had the big 'V' five years ago."

"Beg pardon?"

"The big 'V', a vasectomy."

"You're sure?" she breathed, her knees growing weak.

"I'm one hundred percent sure—so much so, I wouldn't let him dignify such accusations with an answer."

Darby couldn't speak. Her mouth had grown dry and her heart thumped in relief. But Roger must have misinterpreted her silence as suspicion.

"Look, lady, he was a real boob about it. He whined and sniveled and threw up for days—something about the anesthesia caused a reaction and he was put on painkillers for a month. I held his hand through the whole thing, reminding him over and over again that he was a fool for choosing such a method to protect himself from some grasping woman. If he'd had enough control to keep his pants zipped..."

He paused, obviously remembering that Darby had announced herself as a reporter. "Hey, if you don't believe me, give me your name and number. I'll have the doctor fax you a confirmation. I don't want Nick's name even mentioned in connection with Eloise's kid. *Capeesh?*"

Nick Rassmussen wasn't Sissy's father.

It wasn't him.

A jubilation swelled in her chest, and she felt lighter than she had in hours.

"That won't be necessary, Mr. Rassmussen. You can rest assured that I'll keep what you've told me in confidence."

Hanging up the receiver, she took a deep, cleansing breath, then laughed and threw open the phone booth door.

"It wasn't him. He isn't the one! He's not the father!"

Flash.

Darby whirled just in time to find herself face-to-face with a man holding a camera. She froze, unable to believe she hadn't seen him.

Automatically she turned to Christian for help. To her amazement, his hard features cracked in a smile and he started to laugh, really laugh.

He stood, holding the baby in one hand. Taking some money from his pocket, he threw the bills on the table, then grasped the carrier and diaper bag.

The photographer hastily retreated, causing a gust of cool mountain air to hit Darby in the face and rouse her from her stupor.

"Who was that?" she gasped as Christian joined her.

"Probably a reporter." There was no disguising the humor in his voice. "A *real* reporter, not some tabloid journalist."

"Why would you say that?"

"Just a guess. I wouldn't think the paparazzi get to Utah all that often."

Darby scrambled to remember what she'd announced as soon as she'd opened the door to the phone booth. The words swam back to haunt her.

"It wasn't him. He isn't the one! He's not the father!"

She groaned. If that man already knew who she was and pieced together the meaning of her exclamation...

Darby felt a tide of heat climb her cheeks. "What do we do now?"

We. This time she'd been the one to adopt the pronoun.

"What *can* we do?" he responded, lightly. He hooked the diaper bag over her shoulder. "I thought we'd already decided it didn't matter what the media said or did."

"That was before I knew they'd be taking a picture of me with my mouth wide open as I proclaimed that Nick Rassmussen wasn't the father."

Christian laughed again. "Come on. Let's forget about it and investigate the town."

DARBY'S MOOD was unusually somber as they made their way through two specialty shops, the underground jail, the museum and the antiques mall. Wondering why she continued to be so preoccupied with the photographer they'd seen, Christian decided to try another tack in diverting her.

Such a matter would have been easy if Darby had been his ex-wife. He would have steered her toward the closest jewelry store and Rachael's mood would have instantly improved.

But there was no spark of interest in her eyes when they passed the jewelers, or a trendy shoe store. But as soon as they neared a baby boutique...

Bingo!

"Let's go in," he said, taking her arm. He was still holding Sissy since the infant seemed to be mollified by his attention.

To his surprise, Darby balked. "No, I don't think that's a good idea. Sissy has everything she needs."

"So? I thought the whole point of window-shopping was to step inside the actual store now and then."

"I suppose..."

She reluctantly stepped over the threshold, but as soon as she began to investigate the racks of clothing and toys, Christian was amazed at how her discouragement lifted away. Within minutes, he and Sissy were arm deep in ruffles as Darby held one dress up to the baby, then another, then began making a pile of the ones she liked.

"What do you think?"

She held up a dress made of frilly pink and he grimaced.

"Why do women always choose... *that?*"

"What?"

"Girlie stuff."

She offered him a look that told him he'd lost his mind. "Sissy *is* a girl."

"That doesn't mean you have to program her from birth to accept society's stereotypes."

"Beg pardon?"

"In my position as a foreman of engineers, I'm constantly being encouraged to hire women. But the number of women entering the engineering fields is still pretty low—and very few of those females wish to spend a year in the jungle with thirty men."

"What does that have to do with these dresses?"

"Maybe if more little girls had been put in baseball uniforms on occasion instead of frilly pink outfits, they wouldn't *mind* going to the jungle, they wouldn't *mind* being isolated from society, they wouldn't *mind* living so far away from the nearest mall."

Darby stared at him openmouthed. When she spoke, it was to say, "Judging by the deep-rooted paranoia I'm sensing from that statement, this has something to do with your ex-wife?"

Christian shifted uncomfortably. Where in the world had that burst of anger come from? He didn't pine for his ex-wife and he didn't hate women in general. He just...

Avoided them.

Avoided the entanglements they represented.

Until now.

"Sorry," he offered grudgingly, realizing that since joining her, he'd run through more emotions than he'd felt in a long time—surprise, irritation, frustration and humor.

"That's okay," she said, even as she continued to study him. "You like baseball, huh?"

He was grateful for the way she'd changed the subject.

"Which team?"

"The Dodgers."

She grimaced. "I'm a Cleveland Indians fan myself. Anyone who can pull themselves out of the cellar after a strike year deserves my loyalty."

Her remark was enough to startle him, but when she replaced the dresses, selected a tiny Dodgers uniform and took it to the counter, he was completely astonished.

The sun was setting as they loaded the baby equipment into the car and took their places inside. The hotel was less than a mile away, but the parking lot was quiet now that they were out of the main section of town.

As he helped load up the baby and carry her to Darby's room, Christian couldn't help thinking that something had changed between them during their evening together. He realized suddenly that he was regarding Darby as a person instead of a "bride on the run."

He watched as she settled the baby on one of the double beds in her room and surrounded her with pillows. When it became apparent that there was no more need for him to be there, Christian backed toward the door. His hand was on the knob when he turned to say, "You didn't have to do that."

"Do what?" Darby looked up from where she bent over the baby, and in that instant, Christian knew why some men were intrigued by a Madonna-like persona in women. In the dim lamplight, Darby's hair shone like gold and her eyes were dark and luminous.

"You didn't have to buy the Dodgers uniform."

Her grin was instant. "They didn't have one from Cleveland."

He grimaced when she refused to take his comment seriously.

"Just chalk it up to an effort on my part to make the sexes that much more equal," she offered, chuckling. But her laughter died when Christian continued to stare at her, wondering why he'd never really noted her innate beauty until now.

"You're a very lovely woman when you laugh, Darby."

Her smile faded into something far more aware.

"So when I'm serious I'm downright plain?" she countered, but the reply was halfhearted.

"No." He stepped toward her, drawn by some nameless sense of need. "I'm glad you decided to come to Park City by car."

"I'm glad you asked."

"We really did make good time."

"Yes, we did."

"And the baby was so cranky, the plane ride would have been—"

"Impossible."

She nervously licked her lips, and Christian felt a slow flame begin to burn in his belly.

"I appreciate all your help, Christian. If you want, I'll reassure your mother that you kept your word."

Christian shook his head from side to side. "Don't keep thanking me, Darby—and my mother isn't the only reason I offered to help. I'm beginning to believe I had other less altruistic reasons for coming to your aid."

"Oh, really?" Her response was little more than a whisper.

"Yes."

Then, there was no need for words. The quiet told its own story. It thrummed with an intimate awareness that could only be assuaged in one way.

With a kiss.

Christian leaned toward her, his hand cupping her cheek, his thumb stroking her skin.

"Do you want this to happen, Darby?"

He knew exactly what he was asking. If they strayed over the boundary of casual acquaintances, there would be no going back in the future. The strange sort of relationship they'd shared so far would be irrevocably altered. It could no longer be businesslike. Or completely innocent.

But Darby didn't resist him. In fact, she closed half of the distance between them.

Christian's head bent, his lips parting. He felt the warmth of her breath on his cheek and reveled in it. Then, their mouths met, causing a burst of sensation to shimmy through his body.

Her hands lifted to grip his collar, tugging him even closer. She tasted so good, warm and slightly spicy. His arms swept around her waist and she shifted to allow him even more access to her back and shoulders.

How long had it been since he'd held a woman like this? Forever? It had been years since his divorce, but he was sure even Rachael hadn't inspired such an instantaneous desire in him. Darby's kiss made him acutely aware of how many emotions he'd banned from his life. How lonely he'd become. Lonely and hungry and ready for a change.

A change?

A change from what? He would be on his way to Thailand in a few months.

Christian broke free. They both breathed hard, making him wonder if he looked as stunned as she did.

He had to get out of here. He had to leave this woman now, before either of them became involved.

But even as the thought raced through his mind, he found himself asking, "Where's the next candidate?"

"Candidate?"

"For Sissy's father."

It took her a moment to gather her scattered thoughts. "Indiana."

Unable to stop himself, Christian stroked her cheek again.

"I'm heading that way myself, if you'd care to come along."

The minute the words were uttered, he regretted them. Dammit, couldn't he heed his own warnings and leave this woman alone?

"I—I don't know if I..."

She trailed into silence and Christian prepared himself for a refusal.

"Can I wait until morning to give you my answer, Christian?"

He released the breath he'd unconsciously held. "Sure. I'll check on you about nine."

Then he quickly backed from the room before he changed his mind and withdrew his offer.

Chapter Seven

Christian didn't sleep again that night—for several reasons.

First, he castigated himself for extending an invitation to Darby to continue cross-country in his company.

Looking back, he couldn't believe he'd even considered asking her to do such a thing. He was a self-proclaimed loner and this trip had been designed to help him clear his head, decide where he was going in life, what goals he wanted to pursue. Instead he'd spent most of his time with a woman and a squalling baby, which had allowed him no time at all to analyze his future.

After convincing himself that his proposition wouldn't matter because Darby would refuse him outright, there had been his nightly check-in call to his mother. Since she'd seen the home video of Christian and Darby near the wedding chapel, she'd grilled him about how long he and Darby had been friends, how had they met in San Francisco, was he sure he wasn't married? It had taken a good hour to satisfy his mother's fears and hang up the phone.

If that had been his only disturbances, he supposed he might have slept anyway. But very faintly, across the corridor, he could hear the sound of a baby's wail.

Rinsing the shaving cream from his chin, Christian gripped the sink and stared into the mirror. What in hell had got into him? He was the Iron Man. It wasn't any of his business if Darby had spent the night with a fretful baby. He was nothing to her and she was nothing to him. That's the way things should stay. After all, he had a job to do in a couple of months—and heaven only knew he'd tried to maintain a relationship once before by hauling a woman onto the job site with...

Whoa!

Christian straightened, then grabbed the rest of his toiletries and stuffed them in his duffel bag. There was no use entertaining any thoughts about bringing a woman to Thailand, because there was no one special in his life. Just because he'd kissed Darby was no reason to add any special interpretation to the time they'd spent together. He'd been playing the knight in shining armor—at his mother's insistence—that was all.

Grabbing his bag and his check-out receipt—which had somehow been paid in advance by Darby—he shut the door and crossed the hall. Listening carefully, he noted that Sissy wasn't crying anymore, so he tapped lightly with one knuckle.

Darby answered almost immediately. She was dressed in jeans and a loose shirt, her hair combed, makeup applied, but she looked exhausted. Bracing himself, he was sure that she wouldn't be joining him on the road. The next words out of her mouth would be *Christian, I'm sorry, but...*

"Christian, I'm sorry, but I'm not quite ready."

Not quite ready? Did that mean she was going with him, or that she needed a ride to the airport?

When he didn't immediately reply, she shifted uncomfortably.

"Is it all right if I accept your offer of a ride?"

"Of course," he answered quickly, amazed by the relief he felt.

"Sissy's been so cranky lately, I don't want to inflict her on a planeload of people." She flushed. "Of course, I don't want to inflict her on you, either. I just think she'll be happier in a car than on a plane. And you've been so great to put up with us so far—and I really mean that! So I..."

She took a deep breath.

"You're babbling," he commented, then chuckled at her embarrassment.

"I'm sorry."

"Don't be. I'm glad you're coming with me." The moment the words emerged from his mouth, he realized they were true. What surprised him was that he'd freely admitted such a thing.

Her fleeting smile was endearing.

"I'll just get the baby's things together."

Christian stepped into the room. Immediately his attention was drawn to the carrier. Sissy had already been strapped in, but it was obvious she was as exhausted as Darby. Bright spots of color dotted her cheeks and her face was shiny with tears. But what caught and held his attention was the brightly striped baseball uniform she wore and the pseudosneakers that encased her feet. The only real nod to her gender was the bright headband and bow.

For some reason, the sight made Christian smile, and he hooked one finger below the baby's hand until she gripped his knuckle.

"She looks really cute in that getup," Darby commented, gathering her bags. "Bright colors agree with her."

Christian couldn't account for the pleasure the statement brought. "She's a cute kid."

Then, since the mood seemed to be growing too intense, he lifted the carrier and led the way to the car.

THEY WERE ON THE ROAD again within minutes.

Darby still couldn't believe that Christian would allow them to accompany him. She was sure that there were things he wanted to do—things that a woman with a baby might prevent. After all, Christian was a very handsome man. He must have an active social life. A woman in every port.

But he kissed you.

Yes. He had. Even the memory was enough to make her body warm.

Sliding her sunglasses firmly over her nose, Darby studied Christian carefully, taking in his tanned skin, craggy features and dark waving hair.

He was beautiful. There was no other way to describe him. Not pretty-boy handsome, but craggily beautiful with features that could have been hewn from a block of granite. Added to that was a lithe body that bespoke of hard work, and a spirit that was stubborn, yet kind.

She would have given anything to have met him under more normal circumstances. They could have had dinner, talked, gone to a movie. Maybe that way she would have felt more comfortable about asking questions and discovering the real man beneath his show of indifference. Maybe then, she would dare to ask why his ex-wife had made him so bitter. As it was, she felt she should stay with safer subjects. His work and—

And how she would love to run her fingers down his sweat-slick back.

The thought raced through her unconsciousness, taking Darby unawares, causing her to stiffen in reaction as her mind was flooded with inappropriate images.

She'd seen him without his shirt, so there was no denying what she would discover if her fantasy were to become real. But she could only imagine the warmth of his skin. The texture. The sinuous grace of muscles shrouded in copper-colored flesh.

A heat flared to life in her belly, and she resolutely ignored it. Now was neither the time nor the place for such thoughts. Just because she had agreed to his company didn't mean that he planned for anything more to happen.

Or that she should allow anything more to happen.

No.

She mustn't touch him so intimately. Not now. Not ever. She had her own work to contend with, and he had his. Neither of their life-styles would allow for any sort of a relationship to develop. She would accept his offer of a ride and nothing more.

"How long before we make it to Indiana?" Darby asked, pushing the hair away from her brow. The wind immediately blew it back again, and she was glad that she'd recently cut it in a boyish, no-nonsense cut. Granted, Christian had put the top on the car in deference to the baby, but the open windows offered a good deal of ventilation.

Christian considered her question, then countered it with one of his own. "Are you in any sort of rush?"

Rush? Yes. She had to get back to New York and her job. Ricardo hadn't been there when she'd called—who knew where he'd gone with Debbie-what's-her-name.

But until things at the design house hit a crisis point, Darby knew she had to interview the rest of Sissy's possible fathers. If she didn't . . .

You might decide to keep her and damn the consequences.

Even so, she couldn't rush straight to Indiana when part of this trip was supposed to be Christian's. They shouldn't hurry too much. Especially when each minute would mean that much longer with this man. She might actually be able to pin down his enigmatic character. Somehow, she sensed that his "I-don't-give-a-damn'' attitude was only a facade to the much more sensitive person hidden beneath. "No, I'm in no real hurry," she said as casually as she could manage.

"Do you mind if we take things one day at a time then? See the sights, meander through the backroads?"

It sounded like heaven. Sheer heaven.

"I don't mind" was her response, and she congratulated herself on her even tone.

"Good."

He reached across the seat, taking her hand and squeezing the fingers. Darby felt a warmth spread through her skin and ease inward until her whole body was suffused with its sweetness.

"Why are you doing this?" she asked after several minutes.

"Holding your hand?" he retorted.

She cast him a chiding look. "No. Why would you willingly take Sissy and I cross-country to Indiana? The mere thought of such a suggestion would cause any other person to balk at the distance alone."

He shot her several quick glances as he maneuvered the car into a winding canyon that would lead them to Evanston, Wyoming, and from there, further east.

"It beats the hell out of me," he finally said, surprising her with his honesty.

After that, there wasn't much to say, especially since Sissy had begun to cry.

Twisting in her seat, Darby located the baby's pacifier and offered it to the infant, but Sissy adamantly refused to take it in her mouth, shaking her head from side to side. Her hands balled into fists and her face screwed into a fierce grimace.

"There's a rest area up ahead. Near Wanship Dam. I'll pull over so you can hold her."

"Thanks."

Soon the Studebaker had rolled to a stop. Once the tires had ceased crunching in the loose gravel, Darby was unhooking the baby from the car seat and lifting her free.

Darby frowned when she realized that the baby was soaked with perspiration.

"She's burning up," Darby whispered her thoughts aloud.

Christian automatically cupped the baby's head with his broad palm. "She hasn't been that hot before, has she?"

"No. No, she hasn't." Panic flooded Darby like an acrid tide. "What are we going to do, Christian?"

We.

The word had slipped out unconsciously, but she didn't regret it. Not when Sissy's well-being was at stake.

Christian surveyed the area outside of each of the windows and scowled. Their surroundings were far from hospitable. Dun-colored hills spilled down to a dam that had lost too much water over the summer, leaving a muddy waterline and an incongruous row of landlocked docks.

"I think we'd better head straight to Evanston. It's about an hour's drive, but we'd probably have a better chance of locating a hospital or a clinic."

Darby nodded, her throat having grown so tight that she couldn't speak.

As much as it pained her to do so, she placed the baby back in her car seat, then climbed in the back to be near her. As soon as her own seat belt had been fastened, Christian gunned the engine and they were flying onto the highway again.

Within forty minutes, Christian was taking the off-ramp to Evanston, making Darby wonder how many traffic and speed violations he'd broken in the process. The fact that he cared enough about Sissy's well-being to do such a thing warmed her and gave her the strength she needed to endure the last few minutes of waiting.

Following the information signs, Christian took the winding path to the hospital, screeching to a halt near the emergency entrance.

"Come on."

He held open the door, taking the crying baby from her arms, and rushing into the hospital.

To Darby's dismay, the waiting room was already crowded with a variety of sick and wounded people. After signing in and filling out the appropriate forms, they were forced to wait.

Darby was trembling so hard she could barely stand. Seeing this, Christian continued to hold the baby, snuggling her under his chin and swaying from side to side. Darby was amazed at how he appeared so at ease with the child, where days before, he had held her so awkwardly and unemotionally.

Darby's throat tightened and tears stung her eyes. In Christian's arms, the baby had calmed somewhat.

The level of her cries subsided from outrage to a plaintive whimper. Perhaps she sensed the strength of the man who carried her. Or maybe she instinctively knew that he would do his best to make things better.

"Nashton!"

When the nurse called out the baby's last name, Darby stared at her blankly. Nashton? The surname seemed so foreign now, as if the baby weren't a part of Eloise's family at all. If not for the way Christian cupped his hand beneath Darby's elbow and steered her forward, she probably would have remained there, frozen in place.

"You used the baby's real name on the forms, remember?" Christian prompted.

Her real name.

She isn't yours, Darby. She can never be yours.

They were taken to a cubicle dominated by a gurney and a cluster of machinery. The nurse pulled the curtain closed, then took the baby and lay her in the middle of the mattress. Darby shivered, wrapping her arms around her waist and staring down at the red-faced infant. Sissy looked so small on the big hospital bed, so helpless, so sick.

When Christian reached for her, pulling her against his hard length, she didn't resist. She welcomed the heat of his body as it seeped into her own cool flesh. His hands rested on her hipbones, the fingers long and gentle and strong. She had to steel herself so that she didn't lean into him, didn't surrender to him and all he represented.

A man.

A helpmate.

A companion.

The curtain rings shrieked as a doctor wearing a white lab coat laden with collector's pins and political buttons swept into the cubicle. Immediately Darby frowned, wondering if she'd stumbled onto a set of "Doogie Howser M.D." This man—boy, really—looked young, far too young, to be mistaken for any kind of a *real* physician.

"What have we here?" he asked, taking in Darby and Christian at a glance, then focusing on the infant the nurse was undressing.

"The baby became sick while we were on the road," Christian supplied when Darby couldn't bring herself to speak coherently.

"Oh, oh. Do we have a tummy ache?" he asked in a singsong voice.

We. We? Darby had always hated medical professionals who employed the Royal "We" when describing apparent symptoms.

She winced as he rolled the baby onto her side and inserted the rectal thermometer into Sissy's tiny body. It took all the will Darby possessed not to demand that the man show her his credentials here and now.

But after listening to Sissy's chest, examining her ears and *harrumphing* over her temperature, he looped his stethoscope over his neck and pronounced, "She has an inner ear infection."

Darby felt her knees threaten to buckle. "What did I do?" she whispered.

The doctor laughed, his voice cracking. "New mother?" he asked Christian.

Christian's fingers rubbed over her hipbones in an almost imperceptible gesture of encouragement.

"Very new."

The doctor leaned against the gurney as the nurse soothed the baby.

"It's very common in young children, but easily managed with antibiotics. I'd like to give her a shot before she goes, then I'll give you a prescription as well."

"We've been traveling. Will that affect her recuperation?"

The doctor thought for a moment. "Air travel is out of the question for a few days."

Darby nearly wilted again at the thought of how close she and the baby had come to boarding a plane.

"We're in a car," Christian supplied.

"I'd steer clear of some of the higher passes if you can, but—" The doctor stopped, and nudged the nurse, "*Steer* clear. Get it?"

The woman rolled her eyes and handed him a syringe.

He pinched the baby's buttocks and jabbed the needle into Sissy's flesh.

Darby came unglued. How dare he? How dare he be so uncaring, so brutal, so abusive?

But before she could fly at him in a rage, Christian's arm snapped even tighter around her waist.

"That'll do it," the doctor said. "If she doesn't improve in a week or so, give me a call."

Then he was gone, sweeping out of the cubicle as precipitously as he'd come.

"Bastard," Darby growled.

"Hear, hear," the nurse agreed with a grin, then disappeared as well.

Breaking free of Christian's hold, Darby scooped the naked baby into her arms.

"Don't worry, Sissy," she said in a choked voice, scooping the baby's clothes up. "We'll get you dressed and out of here as soon as possible."

BY THE TIME THE BABY had been rediapered and consoled, Darby was so furious she could barely speak. Therefore, it was Christian who scooped the prescription slip from the counter and followed Darby as far as the pharmacy.

"You go ahead. I'll get this filled."

He wasn't even sure if Darby heard him. Her spine grew ramrod stiff as she marched down the corridor and through the automatic doors. As she stomped to the car, he ducked into the pharmacy and extended the prescription to the plump, matronly woman behind the counter.

She lifted a pair of half-moon glasses up to read the scrawling instructions, then dropped them to her ponderous breasts again.

"Ear infection?" she clucked, her lips dragging down at the corners in concern. "How old is your baby?"

Christian shrugged. "I don't know." He held his hands about two feet apart. "She's about this big."

The woman snickered in delight.

"A first-time papa, eh?" she said as she turned away.

First-time papa.

He wasn't an anytime papa.

He wasn't a papa at all.

He was just a ... what?

Friend? Companion? Protector?

Chauffeur?

Feeling suddenly embarrassed and uncomfortable at the whole situation, he tucked his hands into his pockets and pretended to study the racks in front of him. When his brain finally registered that he was staring at a multicolored selection of birth-control boxes, he quickly whirled and made his way to a shelf loaded with baby items.

His eyes widened. There were bottles emblazoned with soda logos, tiny rattles with heads the shapes of animals, socks in all shapes and sizes, itty-bitty spoons, hair ribbons and teething rings. In addition, he saw special fingernail clippers, tweezers, bottle warmers, medicine dispensers, bath thermometers and a dozen kinds of pacifiers.

He'd never known that there were so many things a baby obviously needed. The store he'd entered in Park City had contained clothes and toys, but none of this ... this ... specialized equipment.

One of his fingers nudged a baseball cap that was no bigger than his fist. Emblazoned on the front was the mascot for the Utah Jazz, a furry brown bear.

Funny, but the Jazz had been one of Christian's favorite teams when they'd still been stationed in New Orleans. Since he'd done his undergraduate work in Louisiana, he'd attended at least a dozen games a year.

"If you're looking for the baby Tylenol, it's down a little farther."

Christian started, glancing up at the woman behind the counter.

She made a shooing motion with one finger as if she were prodding a particularly dense child.

"The baby Tylenol will help the fever and make her rest better."

"The doctor didn't say anything about—"

She sniffed. "Dr. Rice is still wet behind the ears, if you ask me. He forgets that new parents weren't given an owner's manual in the delivery room." The finger wagged again. "Baby Tylenol. The drops."

Christian found the appropriate box, then on impulse, snatched the hat from the rack as well. Paying for everything, he asked, "Are there any hotels nearby?"

"You're not from around here?" the woman asked.

"No, ma'am."

"You wait here a minute."

She disappeared into the office, then returned seconds later with a copy of the phone directory. "Most of the places are listed there."

Christian grinned at her. "Thanks."

"Oh, and mister," she called as he passed through the door.

"Yes?"

"You take care of the baby and the missus, you hear?"

She sounded so much like his mother, Christian didn't bother to correct her. "Yes, ma'am, I will," he promised.

As the emergency doors slid closed behind him, Christian's steps slowed. He could see Darby in the back seat of the car, crooning to the baby, but he could not hear Sissy cry.

Surmising that the medicine had kicked in enough to allow the weary baby to sleep, he approached the Studebaker at a more leisurely gait, using the time to study Darby. The "missus."

Missus.

One day she would make some lucky man a wonderful wife. She had such an amazing contrast of personalities—shy one minute, determined the next. She was trusting, yet cautious, alluring and innocent. When the doctor had given Sissy her shot, Christian had thought she would launch across the room and take the man by the throat. Her mothering instincts were incredibly strong.

Perhaps too strong.

Especially for a woman who was doomed to lose the child she'd grown to love.

"Here's the stuff," he said, handing the sack through the window.

Just as he'd thought, Sissy was asleep. Tears streaked her cheeks, and if Christian wasn't mistaken, the same kinds of tracks were etched on Darby's face as well.

Christian cleared his throat of the strange tightness that lingered there. "The instruction sheet says not to start until this evening."

"'Kay."

She *had* been crying. Her voice was thick and gruff. Immediately, Christian wanted to make everything better, but in this case, he didn't know how.

"I also got some baby Tylenol and a..."

He stopped, embarrassed by his impulse purchase.

Darby stared up at him, then opened the sack and offered a soft, "Oh, Christian."

Lifting the hat free, she brushed a thumb over the embroidered bear. "It's wonderful."

Christian shoved his hands into his pockets and peered around him in discomfort.

"I just thought she should have a memento of her first cross-country tour."

"Thank you."

Again, her voice grew husky, and he purposely ignored the fact, knowing that if he comforted her, he would never be able to let her go. Rounding the car, he slid behind the wheel as Darby tucked the sack into the diaper bag, then slid the hat onto Sissy's head. The purple cap, which had seemed so small on the rack, nearly drowned her tiny skull.

"It's so cute. Thank you again, Christian."

Darby sniffed, and Christian looked away, knowing she was on the verge of crying again. Sensing that Darby wouldn't want him to acknowledge her tears, Christian said, "I think we should find someplace to stay in Evanston. At least until we know Sissy is feeling better."

"Yes. I think you're right."

The fact that she didn't argue relayed the depth of her concern for the baby. Normally he knew she would have done everything in her power to keep from "inconveniencing" him.

Slipping the car into gear, Christian quickly oriented himself to the street addresses and referred to the lists of accommodations he'd been given. At the first motel he found that looked clean and inviting, he registered one room. Then, tucking the receipt into his pocket, he drove the car to the appropriate portion of the sprawling building and helped Darby bring the baby and all the infant paraphernalia inside. For some reason he couldn't explain, the baby's belongings seemed to be multiplying, causing several more trips than usual. But finally, they were all ensconced in the room.

One room.

At that moment, Christian realized he hadn't been paying attention. He'd been so concerned about Darby and the baby that he hadn't thought about getting two rooms.

He glanced at Darby, but if she'd caught onto the fact that they would be sharing quarters with him again, she didn't seem to mind.

Crossing to the phone, he punched the appropriate buttons for room service.

"May I help you?" a tired voice answered.

"I want a pot of coffee. Two cheeseburgers, fries and something sweet for dessert. Throw in a couple of colas as well."

After giving the room number, he hung up. Darby had settled Sissy into one of the drawers, and he smiled to himself. *He'd* been the one to give her the idea. But his humor faded when he noted that she still looked panicked and inestimably weary.

Sighing, he took her by the shoulders and pulled her backward.

"She's fine, Darby."

"She's ill."

"But she's sleeping now, and that's the best thing she could do."

He pushed her onto the mattress, then knelt behind her, kneading her shoulders.

Darby's muscles were tense, but bit by bit, they began to shudder and relax.

"I should have taken better care of her."

"Darby," he chided. "Kids get earaches all the time."

"How would you know?"

"The doctor said so."

"That doctor was a bastard. Did you see the way he gave her that shot?"

One of her arms flung out in an accusing gesture and her muscles tensed again.

"Darby, don't," Christian scolded, coaxing the stiffness from her body. "Look how much better she's been just since she had the shot."

He took the ensuing silence as a good sign.

"But Christian, I shouldn't have dragged her willy-nilly over the countryside."

"If you'd taken a plane, things would have been worse."

There was a beat of silence.

"Yes, things would have been worse." Her arm bent and she rested her fingers over his. When she gazed up at him, her eyes were dark and luminous. "You wouldn't have been here to help me."

Christian wasn't sure what he was supposed to say to that, but he didn't bother thinking of a reply. Not when the seriousness of her expression was causing a tightness to spread through his belly and his breath to catch in his throat.

"Don't look at me like that, Darby."

Her features didn't change.

"Why not?"

"Because it's..."

"It's what?" she prompted.

"It's very... disturbing."

"Why?"

He couldn't believe she'd asked such a question. But then, why was he surprised by anything this woman did? From the moment she'd dropped into his life, she'd constantly entertained him with the unexpected.

No. "Entertained" wasn't the word to describe how she'd made him feel. For the first time he could remember, he felt enervated. He looked upon each new day with excitement. He was...

Having the time of his life.

His hand slid beneath her jaw, drawing her up until she knelt on the bed in front of him.

Then he was cupping her face, bringing her to him, hungry, so hungry, for the taste of her.

His lips were greedy as they settled over Darby's, and she moaned, her hands sweeping around his neck, pulling him close, enflaming him even more.

Clutching his hands in the small of her back, he lifted her to his chest, drew her next to his hips, moaning when the softness of her body collided with his chest, his groin.

"Darby," he whispered, then forgot what he'd been about to say.

Her fingers raked through his hair, causing a flurry of gooseflesh to shimmy down his spine. His kiss slanted deeper, his tongue slipping into her mouth to taste her sweetness.

She arched into him even more. The breath expanded in his lungs, growing into an ache, an ache that moved deeper, lower, more insistent.

"Room Service."

The muted call caused the two of them to break apart as if they were teenagers caught by their parents. Darby's face was flushed and Christian waited for her to offer some quick retort that would put them both on an even footing. Instead she looked down, smiling a slow, temptress's smile when she saw the evidence of his arousal.

"I think I'll answer the door. In your condition, it might cause talk."

Quite audaciously, she tunneled her fingers into his pocket, removing the dollar bills that peeked out from the edge.

"I'll take care of the meal charges when we pay for the room, but we'll need this for the tip."

He groaned, sinking onto the bed and leaning his back against the headboard. Suddenly the thought of sharing a room didn't seem to be such a good idea. How was he going to keep his hands off her? Especially when there were two soft, inviting beds. It would be so easy to choose one of them and share.

When Darby returned to the bed, carrying the heavy tray, the thought intensified. Her hair was tousled, her eyes alight with an emotion that he had never seen in a woman before. There was an impish joy, a potent lethargy. A blatant seduction.

"You ordered hamburgers."

Too late, he remembered that he'd never seen her eat meat.

"Yeah."

"Good. I love them."

His heart did an odd little flip-flop. "Really?"

"It's my worst vice where food is concerned. Good greasy cheeseburgers, thick fries and lots of ketchup."

She set the tray in the middle of the bed, then sat cross-legged from Christian. "Too bad you didn't order malts, too."

His brows rose. "My, my. You are living dangerously."

She considered that point. "I suppose I am." She took one of the fries, chewing as she pondered the remark more carefully.

"Those people who knew both Eloise and I never failed to remark that Eloise was the daring one while I was . . ."

"You were what?"

"The stable one." She grimaced. "I always followed the rules and did whatever I was told."

"That's not a bad thing."

"No, but it can be very wearing at times. It takes a great deal of energy to be good."

She ate a sliver of pickle with more sensuality than the action deserved, but Christian knew she was completely unaware of what she was doing.

"I'm very tired of being good, Christian."

"So what would you like to do if you decided to be bad?"

She swirled another fry in the pool of ketchup in the middle of her plate.

"I think I'd run away."

"You're already running away."

She shook her head. "No, I'd *really* run away. I'd take Sissy somewhere and keep her as my own."

The statement shimmered with love. A pure and maternal love that could neither be forced nor denied. Its sincerity was both poignant and powerful.

She offered a shaky laugh as if she'd read a portion of his reaction. "But you don't need to worry about me. Good, old, stable Darby will see to it that the right thing is done." She threw the fry she'd been holding onto her plate. Sobbing, she jumped to her feet and rushed in the direction of the bathroom, but Christian caught her and enfolded her in his arms.

Her body shook and he rocked her from side to side as deep, ragged cries welled from her throat.

"Shh, baby, shh."

Her fingers dug into his shoulders.

"I don't know why I can't let go. She isn't mine. She belongs with her father."

"If you can find him."

"It's only a matter of time," she said forlornly, then began to cry again.

Feeling helpless, he held her even tighter, hoping that some of his warmth would be absorbed by her own chilled flesh. Once again, he wished he had the power to fix things, to give Darby her heart's desire. But as much as he might wish the opposite was true, for Darby's sake, he feared she was right.

Finding Sissy's father was only a matter of time.

Chapter Eight

After the first night in Evanston—when Christian held her, comforted her and eased her into sleep—there was a difference between them, Darby decided. It was as if they'd both exposed a secret to the other's view, an aching vulnerability, and in doing so, they had learned to trust each other at an even deeper level.

They stayed two more days in Wyoming. After the first evening, Darby quickly caught on to the fact that the extra time was for her benefit as much as for Sissy's. Christian was giving her the opportunity to enjoy her role as the baby's guardian. The three of them took long walks, shopped in the touristy boutiques and slept. Darby hadn't realized how tired she'd grown over the past few weeks until she had someone else to share the responsibility of caring for the infant.

Soon however, it was impossible to delay the inevitable. Sissy was growing happy again, her cheeks filling out as she greedily returned to a regular schedule of eating. Even though she balked at taking her medicine, there was no denying that she was feeling better.

Finally, it was Darby who suggested they leave. Within an hour, they were on the road.

"I wish you'd stop paying for the hotel rooms," Christian said as they hit the highway and the speedometer nudged toward sixty-five.

Darby grinned—a very sassy grin that made his stomach tighten and his blood pound.

"I think it's the least I can do."

"The gesture isn't necessary."

"Why not? You won't let me pay for gas, you hardly ever let me pay for the meals. I figure the room is the least I can do—especially since you've helped take care of the baby so much."

Christian grimaced. He'd given the baby a couple of her feedings when Darby was asleep. That was all.

"I'll give you a check to reimburse you once we stop, Darby."

She scowled in mock ferocity. "You will not."

"Darby," he warned.

"What's the matter? Are you afraid someone will think you're a kept man?"

He gazed at her in astonishment. "You have quite the mouth, don't you."

"Why? Because I'm the only woman other than your mother who dares to resist your bulldozing techniques?"

"I do not use bulldozing techniques."

"Spare me the innocent routine, Christian. I heard you talking to one of your foremen on the phone."

Christian glanced at her, then back at the road.

"The poor man was shaking in his shoes by the time you finished with him, I'm sure. And all because of a partial order."

"I need that order for Thailand."

"Of course you do. And I'm sure you'll have it, too. Your foreman wouldn't dare disobey you."

Christian fought the grin tugging at his lips. "But you do, huh?"

"Of course." She poked him in the arm with a finger. "I've seen the real Christian Drake. The one who secretly stole Sissy's rubber duck and—"

"Once. I took it once to see if the blasted thermometer built inside the thing would really measure the temperature of bathwater."

"And did it?"

"Yes," he admitted grudgingly.

Darby laughed, and even though he knew he shouldn't, Christian joined in.

"Like I said, Christian. That old Iron Man routine won't work with me."

He stared at her in amazement. How in the world had she known about his nickname?

But when he decided to ask, she reached back to adjust Sissy's blanket and the moment was lost.

Later, he told himself. They had all the time in the world to talk.

"BUT RICARDO HAS TO BE THERE, Jean-Paul."

"And I am telling you he is not, *chérie*," a weary, French-laden voice returned. "We 'ave not seen him in days."

"Damn."

"When will you be back, Dar-bee?"

Jean-Paul always had the ability to make her name sound very exotic, but this time she wasn't able to enjoy the fact.

"I should be in Indiana sometime tonight. After that, I'll have more of an idea of my timetable."

Jean-Paul sighed. "Some decisions 'ave to be made."

Darby inhaled, knowing that Jean-Paul was right.

"Go ahead and cut the designs, Jean-Paul."

She could feel the man's tension over the phone. "You're sure?"

"We can't delay any longer. Not if we're going to be ready for the show."

"Very well. I will give the order."

Darby slowly replaced the receiver, wishing she wasn't giving such important orders over the phone. She should be there, overseeing the entire process—especially if Ricardo was pulling a disappearing act. But until she could get back...

Sighing, she ran back to the waiting car and climbed inside.

"Problems?"

"Yes. My boss is still gone and we're to a point where the clothes have to be put into production." She bit her lip, then said, "I told them to start cutting the designs."

"Do you trust your staff to do the best possible job?"

She glanced at Christian in surprise. "Of course."

"Are your people reliable?"

"Incredibly."

"Then don't worry about what's happening at work."

She blinked at him in surprise. "Somehow, I wouldn't have expected such a philosophy to spout from your lips."

"Why not?"

"You seem to be a very 'hands-on' kind of guy."

The moment the words were uttered, she wished she could retrieve them. In the limited space of the car, her statement sounded too much like a come-on.

Christian gazed at her for several heart-wrenching minutes, then he pulled the Studebaker onto the highway.

"I guess I am a hands-on kind of guy." His voice was so low, she almost didn't hear it. Then he changed the subject so quickly, she had trouble keeping up. "Why did you call me the Iron Man?"

"What?"

"When we left Wyoming, you referred to me as the Iron Man."

Darby tried to remember the incident, but couldn't. "I don't know. I suppose I said the first thing that popped into my head. Why?"

Christian didn't seem inclined to answer right away, but finally said, "My crew used to call me that."

She couldn't help but smile. In her mind's eye, she could see Christian shouting orders from the top of a bridge's iron framework.

"You must be a real bully on the job."

Again he searched her features, then returned his attention to the road. Something about his quick scrutiny caused her to ask, "That's why you earned the nickname, isn't it?"

The whine of the tires punctuated the moment of silence before he said, "No."

"Then why?"

He flexed his fingers around the wheel. "Because I have a reputation for being a woman-hater."

He could have opened her door and pushed her out and Darby wouldn't have been more surprised. Christian Drake? A woman-hater?

"Why in the world would they think that?"

Again he gripped the steering wheel. "When my crew heads into town for recreational purposes I . . . stay behind."

Darby met his quick gaze, and knew instantly what nuances were hidden behind his succinct statement. "Just because you choose not to . . . buy a woman's affection—" despite the euphemism she employed, her cheeks still grew hot "—that doesn't make you a woman-hater. It just means you're more discerning in your choices."

Again he looked at her, his eyes hot.

"Are you sure?"

His deep query had the ability to send gooseflesh racing down her spine.

"Yes, I'm sure."

"So what does that make you, Darby? Other than my sisters, you're the first woman I've spent time with since my divorce."

Darby couldn't speak as the importance of his statement hit her like a lightning bolt. She offered him a saucy shrug as her answer.

But the little voice in her head replied, *It makes you a damned lucky lady, that's what.*

THEY ARRIVED in the small town of Wellington, Indiana, just before dusk. The moment she saw the sign announcing the city limits, Darby's stomach began to tie in knots. As much as her mind was beginning to dwell on thoughts of Christian, she had business to conduct in this place.

"What do you plan to do now that we're here?" Christian asked.

Darby sat still, her hands clasped in her lap. "I think it would be best if I talked to Alec Davinci right away."

Christian searched her expression. "You're sure?" he asked. When she remained silent, he took her hand, squeezing it in reassurance.

She nodded, knowing that it was the right thing to do. "Yes. I've got to see him tonight before I lose my nerve."

"Or he catches an episode of 'The Gossip Exchange,'" Christian quipped.

Since the reporter in Park City, the two of them had become a regular segment on the show, a fact that had become a running joke between them.

Squinting through the rain that was pelting the windshield faster than it could be wiped away, she grabbed Christian's arm.

"Stop!"

"Where?"

"At that beauty shop up ahead."

He complied, staying in the car with the baby as she dashed inside, holding a newspaper over her head to shield herself from the pounding rain. When she returned minutes later, his brows climbed.

"What was that all about?"

"You'll see."

CHRISTIAN CHOSE the only hotel with a vacancy. As they pulled into the parking lot and Darby dashed into the office, he surveyed the architecture of the establishment. He guessed the lodgings had been built some time in the thirties when motor touring was at its highest because the rooms had been built to resemble miniature houses strung together with common porches.

His fingers drummed against the back of his seat, and Sissy giggled, reaching out her hands as if to catch the wriggling shapes she saw.

Christian grinned, leaning back to tickle the baby under her chin. She erupted in a spurt of laughter, a sound that had grown more and more common as her health had improved and Christian had discovered her ticklish spots.

He nudged her again and was rewarded by a damp rivulet of drool.

"Sheesh, kid," he said, wiping her chin with the burp cloth. "You've got to learn how to turn off the waterworks."

Sissy squealed in delight, and Christian couldn't help laughing himself. With each day that passed, he was discovering that a female didn't have to be fully grown to wrap a man around her little finger. In fact, he would go so far as to say that babies, especially this one, knew some sort of magic spell. They attracted a person's attention with a grin or a sigh, and then it was impossible to look away.

The passenger door opened and Christian started as if his thoughts hung visibly in the air.

"They only had one room," Darby announced as she climbed inside. "There's a clogging convention in town."

He stared at her blankly. "Clogging?"

"You know, the stuff that looks like some sort of Western tap-dance routine."

As the information sank into his brain, Christian grew very still, his body filling with an electric tension. Since Wyoming, he and Darby had never shared a room. Rather, they'd shared a tacit understanding that spending too much time in the same hotel room could lead to some serious emotional complications.

"Is that all right?" Darby asked tentatively.

No. He shouldn't share a room with her. Not now. Not ever.

"Sure. If they don't have two spots, they don't have two spots."

"We're over there. Number three." Darby pointed to the first bungalow.

Christian parked the car and they quickly unloaded the belongings they would need for the evening.

As soon as the baby was settled, Darby disappeared in the bathroom and Christian stretched out on one of the beds. Staring resolutely at the flickering television screen, he did his best to ignore the fact that Darby had taken a change of clothing and the bag of beauty supplies with her. Resolutely he kept his mind off the patter of the shower and the soft feminine humming.

But when the door opened and she emerged, he couldn't help looking.

"What do you think?" she asked, taking a vampish pose.

Christian stared at the black flats, black jeans, crisp oxford shirt, and carefully applied makeup. But what caught and held his attention was her hair. It was black. Coal black.

"What the hell happened to you?"

She grinned. "It's my reporter disguise."

Christian tried to remain open-minded—especially since such a role had been his own idea—but he felt the muscles in his face grow grim. "You dyed your hair?"

"No, silly. It's a wig."

His breath escaped in a rush of relief.

"Do we have a phone book?" Darby asked as she bounded across the room.

He pointed to a nightstand where the directory hung from a mangled chain.

She quickly looked up Davinci's name, and was pleasantly surprised to find it listed.

"Well?" Christian asked.

"It's here."

Her voice was quiet. Too quiet. Too telling.

She didn't want to meet this man. She didn't want him to be Sissy's father.

Since she didn't seem inclined to move, he asked, "Are you going to call?"

She didn't respond.

"Darby?"

"Yes. Yes, I'm going to call."

The baby began to fuss and Christian scooped her into his arms, jiggling the baby and automatically offering her the pacifier that was attached to her rompers by a length of grosgrain ribbon. The baby immediately grew quiet, grinning up at him as if she had performed an amazing trick.

She reached for the phone, then hesitated. "Am I doing the right thing?"

Christian knew what she meant. "You said her mother wanted Sissy to live with her biological father."

"Yes, but are blood ties enough? Aren't other things just as important? Doesn't she belong with someone who will rock her when she has an earache and teach her how to pull faces?"

"How do you know her father won't do those things if you never give him a chance?"

Darby remained frozen in place.

"Darby?"

Christian's prompting caused her to start.

"Sorry," she mumbled as she looked at the numbers in the directory. Her hand shook as she punched the numbers. After three rings, a low, gruff voice responded.

"Alec Davinci, here."

DARBY STIFFENED. She hadn't expected the man to answer in person.

"Mr. Davinci, my name is Randa Bolivar."

Christian's eyebrows arched at the pseudonym and she had to turn away from him to keep from breaking character. "I work for a European magazine."

"Oh, really," Alec Davinci drawled with evident interest.

"Yes. I'm doing a story on Eloise Nashton."

There was a pause on the other end. "She died, you know."

"Yes, I know." Darby cleared her throat. "The accident was so tragic, especially considering the manner of her death, so my editor has asked me to do a feature on her life, her personal acquaintances and her business associations. I believe you were acquainted with Ms. Nashton."

She heard a grunt.

"She was a close friend, actually."

Close? How close?

"Could I ask you some questions?"

Again, he hesitated. "Sure. But not here."

There was a call from the background, a muffled conversation, then he returned to say, "I was about to join some of my crew for a game of pool at the Bucket O' Suds on Decatur. I'll meet you there in say...thirty minutes."

The line went dead before Darby could say anything more.

"Well?" Christian asked when her silence continued.

"We need to meet him in town."

"Where?"

"A place called Bucket O' Suds. It's on Decatur."

Christian frowned. "This doesn't sound good. It doesn't sound good at all."

"What do you mean?"

"It sounds like a bar."

"It is a bar. He's going to be playing pool with some friends."

"Don't you think you could find somewhere less public?"

Darby rose and straightened her wig. "I think a public place will be perfect for our needs. That way, he can't make too much of a fuss." She grabbed the diaper bag. "Let's go."

A LAYER OF SMOKE hung heavy in the bar, combining with the pungent smell of old beer and the *thump, thump, thump* of the honky-tonk music blaring from the corner jukebox.

"This place is awful," Darby whispered the moment her eyes had scanned the room, but her words were lost long before they could reach Christian's ears. "Maybe you should wait in the car with the baby, Christian."

"Not on your life."

He was glaring at the sawdust on the floor, the ripped vinyl seats of the booths and the bar littered with sticky puddles and peanuts.

"This isn't the sort of place for a baby," Darby shouted in order to be heard.

"It isn't the sort of place for either one of you!" he shouted back.

Darby couldn't prevent the thrill she felt at his evident concern.

"Take that booth over there," he said, gesturing to one in the corner that was relatively clean. "I'll stay here by the door. If there's any trouble, I'm taking you out of here."

Darby supposed she should object and insist that she could take care of herself, that she was a modern woman accustomed to the hazards of the singles' world, but she didn't. Right now, she was happy to have some sort of "backup."

"Twenty minutes," she said. "If he isn't here by then, we can wait outside."

"Fine."

She slid into the booth, grimacing when a ragged piece of vinyl snagged her jeans. With her luck, she'd probably ruined the hose beneath, which meant she'd be making another trip to the store.

Adjusting the dark wig, which was beginning to itch, she took a pad from the voluminous purse she'd bought on the way, a pen and a mechanical pencil, wishing she had a tape recorder so that she looked even more official.

"What can I get you?"

She jumped, glancing at the rotund bar keeper who had draped a soiled dishcloth into his waistband to form a makeshift apron.

"Coffee."

"We don't got no coffee. It's broke."

Darby wasn't sure exactly what was broken, but she wasn't about to ask.

"A diet soda, please."

"What kind?"

"Surprise me."

The man's grizzled brows climbed, but she saw a sparkle to his eyes as if he was pleased by her audacity—as well as her bravery.

"I'll do that."

As he ambled away, Darby busied herself with her paper and pen, writing Alec Davinci's name, the date, the time.

Hurry, hurry, hurry.

She looked at Christian, at the door, at the baby.

Hurry, hurry, hurry.

"Here."

She jumped when the bartender returned and set a tall glass on a folded napkin.

The man chuckled when she eyed the glass suspiciously. "Relax. It's a diet cherry cola."

This time, her brows were the ones to rise. "That sounds wonderful."

"Give it a try."

She dutifully sipped the drink, nearly sighing aloud when the sweet cherry syrup combined with the sparkling cola slid over her tongue. "This is marvelous."

"It's the cherries. I don't use maraschinos, they can be bitter sometimes. I use black cherries—put 'em up myself from a tree that grows back of the bar. The canning recipe is over fifty years old, just like my mother used to make during the Depression. Don't have many people who appreciate such a touch at the Bucket."

"You should patent the stuff. You'd make a million."

His eyes twinkled and the stiffness eased from his stance. "Maybe so. But I don't think it would be worth having my mother come back to haunt me for commercializing her secret concoction."

Darby chuckled. "That may be true." She took another sip. "So I suppose I'll have to enjoy it while I can."

The man touched a finger to his brow in silent salute, turned as if to leave, then paused and added, "We certainly don't get many women like you here."

The comment was given in a way that encouraged more conversation, and it was at that moment Darby realized that Wellington was a small town. Like most small towns, she'd bet that everyone knew everyone else—and who would know more than the owner of the corner bar?

Sensing that this man was a teddy bear beneath his gruff layer of cynicism, she gestured to the opposite seat.

"Why don't you join me?"

It was obvious that he'd never had such a request.

"Please," she urged. "If someone needs you, I'm sure they'll holler. In the meantime, I'd love the company."

He hesitated, then hooked his foot around a chair leg and drew it close to the booth where she sat. "Just fer a minute," he warned.

"Just for a minute."

His eyes narrowed beneath enormous, bristled brows. "Are you some kind of reporter?"

Darby fought the urge to grin. The disguise must have been better than she thought.

"What if I am?" she countered.

"It would explain a lot."

She stirred the ice in her drink with her straw. "Such as what?"

"Why you came in with that guy," he said with a jerk of his head, "then left him at the door. Paparazzi do that to throw off suspicion, then they start taking pictures."

Her own gaze skipped to Christian who was slouched in a chair, the baby settled in his lap, her Utah Jazz ball cap pulled low over her eyes as if she needed her own brand of disguise.

"You're very observant."

"I also figure you're after some sort of interview with Alec. We get somebody in here at least once or twice a week."

"Really?" She looked at the bartender in astonishment. "I didn't realize racers were so much in demand."

"They are in these parts."

"You must have grown good at spotting outsiders, then."

"I have to be. It's part of my job."

"I suppose it's also your job to know your customers really well."

"I know enough about the regulars."

"Is Alec Davinci a regular?"

"Like clockwork," the man said with a certain edge of bitterness. "I wish I could claim otherwise. Sally deserves to have someone home nights."

"Sally?"

"His wife."

The man had a wife.

"She's got her hands full with the twins."

The man had twins.

"Twins?" She gulped.

"Yeah, they were born about a year ago. The town made quite a fuss over the kids, considering Alec and Sally had been married for well over a dozen years before the babies came along."

Darby's stomach had begun to do sick flip-flops and she took a gulp of her drink. "A... *dozen* years?"

"Mmm-hmm. Those two babies were quite a miracle—especially considering how they got here."

Darby took another sip of her drink. "How *did* they get here?"

The bartender looked over each shoulder as if he were being overheard, then said, "Well, y'see, Alec was injured in the Indianapolis 500 about fourteen years ago. It was one of the first races he ever did. It wasn't his fault. The guy ahead of him blew a tire, lost control and careened into the wall, taking Alec with him. Anyway, Alec had some bad injuries." His voice lowered even more. "So bad, they had to remove one of his... you know."

Darby didn't know, but when the bartender made a couple of sliding glances toward his own lap, she suddenly understood.

"How awful." She shuddered.

"I guess the other... well, you know, was damaged, too, because he was cursed with some slow swimmers. He and Sally finally ended up going to an expensive clinic in Virginia. The doctors there harvested Alec's sperm, then Sally was artificially inseminated.'' He snorted. ''I guess the little fellers swim better in packs.''

Even Darby was forced to laugh, but sobered immediately when she realized that she still had some detective work to do.

''Mister...''

''Call me Cabby.''

''Mr. Cabby, have you ever seen this woman?''

She took out her day-planner and flipped to the photographs she kept in the back.

''Why, that's Ms. Nashton!'' Cabby cried, pulling the picture close. ''She was a friend of Sally's. She came to stay with Sally just after the twins were born—I guess the two of them met about a year before that, during one of Alec's races. According to Sally, Ms. Nashton was baby-hungry—especially once she came to visit the Davincis. 'Course, I guess the fact that she was expecting herself might have had something to do with it.''

''She was expecting?'' Darby breathed.

''I think Sally said Ms. Nashton was in the first few weeks, so she didn't want to announce anything. But I remember how Ms. Nashton headed straight for the rest rooms as soon as she entered the bar.''

''Had she seen the Davincis before that time? In the weeks before then?''

''Doubt it. Sally and Alec were both wrapped up in their babies at first. For six weeks Alec rarely left home— Alec even canceled a race so that he could be home.''

So the likelihood that Alec Davinci was Sissy's father was slim to none.

Darby finished her soda, suddenly buoyant and ready to leave.

"Thank you, Cabby." She began to gather her things. "When Mr. Davinci comes in, will you tell him I've changed my mind about the interview?"

Cabby was clearly astounded. "Why?"

"I meant to ask some rather...personal questions. But after listening to you, I think I'll leave Mr. Davinci to his privacy."

Cabby grinned in approval. "That's right nice of you, ma'am. Most reporters don't have a conscience."

Darby felt like a worm. She *didn't* have a conscience. If she did, she wouldn't be skulking around bars dressed like a reporter, looking for a man with viable sperm.

"Thank you again, Cabby," she said after placing some bills on the table.

"Anytime, Miss. Come in again for a black cherry cola."

"I will."

She hurried to the exit, not even pausing as Christian rose to join her and held the door open to let her pass. Once outside, she took deep gulps of fresh air.

"What's wrong?"

She whirled, grinning. "It isn't him."

"Are you sure?"

"Sure enough."

"What is that supposed to mean?" Christian demanded.

"I'll tell you later."

"Darby," he warned, obstinately planting his feet in the gravel and refusing to budge. "What the hell happened in there?"

On impulse, she wrapped her arms around his neck, enclosing him and the baby in her embrace. "Alec Davinci had an accident that made him all but incapable of conceiving without medical intervention." She leaned close, rubbing her lips over his jaw. "Other than that, the timing isn't right. Eloise was already pregnant when she saw him the last time."

He held the baby with one arm and the other wound around her waist.

"It isn't him," he murmured, and she was touched by the relief she heard in his own voice.

"That's what I've been trying to tell you," she said, her lips inching closer to his. "She's ours, Christian," she whispered. "Even if it's only for a few more days, she's still ours."

Then she was kissing him, communicating with her body and her desire the things she was still too afraid to admit to herself—how much she'd grown to depend upon him, how much she'd grown to care for him.

The passion was instantaneous, ignited by too many days on the road together.

Darby's hands cupped the back of Christian's head, her fingers raking through his hair as she had wanted to do on so many occasions. She'd spent so many hours denying herself of just such freedoms, that to indulge them now set her heart and her body aflame.

Finally it was the crunch of tires on gravel that split them apart.

Christian grabbed her by the wrist, pulling her to the Studebaker. "Come on," he rumbled, his voice throbbing with a retained desire.

"Where are we going?" Darby gasped.

He fastened Sissy in her car seat, then opened the door for Darby, but did not allow her to sink onto the seat. Instead he kept her in the lee of space he'd created, shielding her from view from the customers that had arrived, but pulling her body flush with his.

"Where do you want to go?"

The question shuddered in the darkness, filled with a rich promise of sensual delight.

She shivered in reaction, gripping his shirt at his waist, wanting to pull him closer, but knowing that things were going much too quickly for them both.

"I want..."

But she couldn't finish the sentence. She didn't dare.

His head dipped, his lips resting against the shell of her ear and causing gooseflesh to race from that point all the way down to her toes.

"What do you want, Darby?"

She made an unintelligible mewl of distress. To say the words aloud, to admit her raging desire for this man would be far too brazen. Too soul-baring.

Gazing up at him, she tried to communicate a measure of her distress, knowing that if he urged her to tell him the truth one more time, she would not be able to refuse him. Nor would she be able to refuse the consequences such a confession would bring.

Christian cupped her cheek, tipping her head toward the light of the street lamp. She saw his own fierceness, his own craving. Then, just as surely, she saw it ease and the understanding flood through him.

"It's too soon," he murmured.

She nodded, unable to speak.

"But if we continue on as we have, the time will come when we'll reach this point again."

"I know."

It was an admission of their mutual desire.

Their mutual regard.

He smiled at her, even though the smile was rife with his own self-deprecation.

"You have a powerful effect on a man, Darby Simms."

She shook her head. "No. I only have that effect on you."

The statement was so audacious, she couldn't believe that she'd uttered the words aloud. But when he grinned and chuckled aloud, she was glad that her instincts had led her down the right path.

"Get into the car before I ravish you, woman," he groused good-naturedly.

Sliding onto the seat, she checked to be sure Sissy was securely fastened in her car seat while Christian took his own place behind the wheel.

As he gunned the engine, she asked, "Where shall we go?"

Unspoken between them was the suggestion that it was still too soon to return to the hotel. A hotel with very limited quarters. Soft beds. Clean sheets. Dim lighting.

"You once said you had a thing for malts," Christian began.

"So?"

"So I saw an old-style hamburger drive-in on the outskirts of town. What do you say we find the place and order over-the-top malts."

Once again, Darby was reminded of all the good habits she'd developed over the past few years, the careful elimination of fat from her diet, the increase of fiber and exercise.

But looking into Christian's molasses-warm eyes, she realized that a lot of her old habits were suffering a meltdown. She wasn't quite as rigidly obedient to the rules she'd made for herself as she'd been only weeks before. The freedom was incredibly enervating.

And enticing.

"You're on, Drake," she murmured. "I'll even chip in for an order of fries."

Chapter Nine

The hamburger joint was bursting with cars and teenagers. Darby watched in delight as young girls—and a few boys—wearing roller skates and fifties attire, waited on the customers with a speed that defied explanation. It was less than five minutes after their order that Christian and Darby received two huge glasses piled with an ice-cream concoction that was so thick it proved impossible to drink through a straw. That, combined with a basket of steaming fries filled the car with the redolent smells that brought back memories of sneaking out of school with Eloise and making their way into town for some fun.

Soon, however, they began to notice that the other cars were leaving as soon as they received their food.

"What's the rush?" Christian asked when their carhop rolled by and inquired if their food had been prepared properly.

"The drive-in theater is showing a John Wayne marathon."

Christian's expression immediately brightened. "You've got a drive-in theater around here?"

"Sure." She pointed to a distant grove of trees that bloomed inky black against the darkening sky. "Head on down the lane and turn left at those trees. Just beyond those hills, you'll see all the lights.

Christian turned to Darby. "How about you? Are you game for an all-night movie marathon?"

Since the alternative was spending the night in the hotel room ignoring each other, she readily agreed.

Signaling to the carhop, they exchanged the metal cups for paper ones and the plastic basket of fries for a sack. Then they were barreling down the road, following a ribbon of cars with flashers that blinked like a string of cheerful Christmas lights.

After paying for their tickets, Christian pulled up to one of the silver mike stands, and placed the small speaker on the half-rolled window.

Darby laughed in delight. "Everyone is staring at your car."

"It belongs in a setting like this, doesn't it?"

"All I need is a poodle skirt and a cashmere sweater."

He waggled his brows in mock wolfishness. "Mmm. Cashmere."

Giggling, she released her own seat belt, loosened the strap securing the sleeping baby and slouched down in her seat.

"Are you a fan of John Wayne's?" she asked when the lights around the parking lot flickered in warning.

"Sure, aren't you?"

She shrugged. "I've never seen one of his pictures."

He stared at her as if she'd bloomed another head. "You're kidding, right?"

She shook her head. "You're forgetting. I spent most of my adolescence in a girls' school."

"What about reruns on television and late night movies?"

She shrugged. "Somehow, I never got around to John Wayne, I guess."

"Well, it's time we augmented your education," he said with such seriousness that she nearly believed his seriousness was real. "Tonight you're in for the best of the best. *McLintock,* followed by *True Grit,* then *Donovan's Reef.* If you're up to it, we might even stay for *Rooster Cogburn.*"

The titles were unfamiliar to her, but she enjoyed Christian's enthusiasm and the way his eyes sparkled as he talked about the movies.

"I take it that you've seen them all dozens of times?"

"Sure. My dad loved a good Western. He'd take the kids to the theater as soon as a John Wayne movie hit town."

"Kids? You have several brothers and sisters?"

"Sure."

She was astounded. For some reason, she'd assumed that he was a loner through and through. She'd never considered the fact that Christian had siblings.

"Why haven't you ever mentioned them?"

He shrugged. "I don't know. I've called them a couple of times since we've been on the road."

She would have given anything to have been privy to those conversations. To have heard what he'd said about her.

"So they know that you're traveling cross-country with me?" she asked carefully, not wanting to tip her hand that she cared what his family thought about the situation.

Even though she did care.

More than she ever would have thought possible.

He made a soft snorting sound. "My mother passed the news on first thing. My younger sister was immediately concerned about a car seat. I promptly informed her that we'd taken care of that item. My older brother, on the other hand, was worried about gas mileage with the Studebaker."

"Where do they live?" she finally managed to ask.

"My brothers and sisters are scattered throughout the country, but my parents live in New York state. I thought if we got that far, we'd drop by for a visit."

If we got that far.

The words echoed in her ears. If they followed a trail of daddy candidates, there would be no reason to go to New York. Her next stop was Kentucky, then Louisiana, then Virginia.

"I don't think they'd want to meet me," she finally said, looking away and stirring what was left of her malt with her spoon. Suddenly she wished she hadn't eaten so much. The food lay in her stomach like a lump of lead.

Christian touched her chin, forcing her to meet his gaze.

"What makes you say that?"

"I'm sure they think I'm some sort of flake."

"Why?"

"Because I latched onto their son and forced him to drive cross-country."

"You didn't force me to do anything." His lips tilted to one side in a cockeyed grin. "If anything, they're a little in awe of you."

"Of me?"

"Sure. I've always been the rebel of the family. I rarely stay in one spot for more than a year or two, let alone settle my attentions on one woman. They think it's a miracle that you've managed to intrigue me for—what has it been? A week? Ten days?"

"Thirteen." She knew because she'd counted each minute. Each hour.

"See? You now hold the world record in my parents' book."

"And have I?" she asked breathlessly.

"Have you what?"

"Have I captured your attention? Or are you merely sorry for my predicament?"

His hand shifted, cupping her behind the head and pulling her closer. "I am not sorry for you, Darby," he said fervently. "If anything, I feel sorry for all the men who must have let you go."

Then he was kissing her, his lips warm and gentle and probing. She leaned into him quite willingly, absorbing his warmth and his adoration.

But when she would have deepened the caress, he drew away, settling her into the crook of his arm and resting her head on his shoulder.

"That's enough for tonight."

She smiled, secretly pleased by the ragged tone of his voice and the irregular thumping of his heart beneath her ear.

"Why?" she boldly inquired, even though she knew the answer.

"Because we're steaming up the windows of a Studebaker in a drive-in—and that fact alone has to be responsible for at least a portion of the baby-boomer population."

She laughed, her hand sliding across his waist. The hiss of his indrawn breath made her own heart complete a drunken flip-flop.

"I'll behave if you will."

He moaned. "Just keep your eyes on the screen, all right?" he urged.

"Fine. I'll keep my eyes on the screen."

To her infinite surprise, she enjoyed the movies— each and every one. She laughed through *Mc-Lintock*'s antics, cringed at *True Grit*'s snakes, and railed at *Donovan's Reef*'s open sexism. But midway through *Rooster Cogburn* it began to rain. Even though Christian turned on the wipers, the spattering drops began to hypnotize her and lull her into a cocoon of sleep. Vaguely she felt Christian starting the engine, then the hiss of the tires on the road, but her contentment was too deep to disturb.

When he carried her into the hotel room and lay her on the bed, she roused enough to catch his hand.

"I had...wonderful time..." she sighed, noticing out of the corner of her eye that Sissy was flailing and gurgling in her baby carrier, which he'd set on the dresser.

She thought she felt his lips brush her cheek, thought he smiled against her.

"Me, too," he said.

Then she surrendered completely to oblivion.

CHRISTIAN WATCHED her snuggle deeper into her pillow and tug the covers beneath her chin. At that moment, she didn't look much older than a kid herself.

But she wasn't a kid, he thought again when his gaze slid to the firm breasts plumped beneath the blanket, the tiny waist, the swelling hips.

She was a woman through and through.

Knowing that if he stayed where he was for much longer, she wouldn't get her rest at all, he backed away, lifting the baby from her carrier.

He fixed the formula with the practiced efficiency of a professional, then settled onto the bed, resting his back against the headboard.

"What would you like to watch tonight, Sissy?" he asked as she greedily downed the bottle. "A movie? Ah! Sports highlights."

On the television screen, a montage of football and baseball clips flashed past, but they failed to hold his interest. Even though he knew it was dangerous to his own emotional sanity, Christian found himself observing the baby, the fuzz of hair at the top of her head, her grunts of pleasure, the tiny flailing hands with their incredibly detailed lines and creases.

"You are indeed a miracle, aren't you, Sissy?" he asked, taking the bottle.

Before he could even lift her, she offered him a heartfelt belch.

"I'll take that as an agreement," he said chuckling. As a matter of habit, he reached for the phone and punched out a familiar series of numbers.

The other end rang once, twice, then was answered by a sleepy voice.

"Hello?"

"Hi, Ma, it's Christian."

He heard a quick chortle. "Who else would it be?"

In the background there was a grunt and a muffled exchange of words. Christian could nearly see his father being roused from sleep, then rising to push his feet into the same moccasin slippers Christian had sent him from his summer camp crafts class twenty years before.

"I'm on the extension, Nan," Robert called needlessly.

"Hi, Dad."

"How are the tires holding out?"

"Just fine, Pop."

"Are you keeping the baby warm?" his mother asked.

"I'm feeding her right now."

"Make sure you burp her."

"She's already done her part, Mom."

"So tell us what you've been up to today, boy," Robert urged.

From that point, it was no trouble at all to slip into the familiar routine of Robert and Nan Drake's son. Even so, there was a difference, Christian realized.

He'd changed in the past few days.

But how long-lasting that change proved to be was still a mystery.

IT WAS DAWN when Christian awoke with a start. Automatically he looked at the baby and found her sleeping. But when his eyes strayed in Darby's direction, he encountered an empty bed.

Sliding into his jeans, he yawned and padded to the bathroom, but the door was open, the room empty.

His brow creased and he moved back into the main room. A glance at the clock on the nightstand proclaimed five-thirty. *Five-thirty?* No one sane was up at this hour of the morning if he had a choice in the matter. Where could she be?

Opening the door, Christian found Darby huddled beneath the porch overhang of the motel, staring out at the pounding rain. She didn't appear to notice him as he joined her, his bare feet making little noise on the concrete.

"What's wrong?"

She jumped slightly when he spoke, but didn't turn to face him.

"One more candidate down," she murmured.

"Three to go."

He knew she didn't need the reminder, but he felt bound to fill the silence with something other than the drumming rain.

"Christian?"

"Hmm?"

"Have you ever wished you had a child of your own?"

The question was so innocent on the surface, how could she possibly know what sorts of memories it would rouse? How could she possibly know, that after speaking with his parents, he'd found himself wishing that he had his own son. Or a daughter. Like Sissy.

"I thought I was going to be a father once."

She regarded him curiously.

"I was barely out of high school when the girl I'd been dating for some time told me she was pregnant."

Darby's mouth opened in a small *o*.

"I asked her to marry me. We eloped, sneaking over state lines and she became Mrs. Christian Drake."

Darby was quite clearly stunned.

"But you aren't a father," she whispered. "I mean, you didn't know what to do with a baby until Sissy came along."

"No, I'm not a father. It was all a lie. Rachael wanted to get away from the environment she had at home, and she thought I was the answer. Because I was intent upon becoming an engineer, she was sure that she would be married to a rich man." He dug his fingers into his pockets. "Two years after I earned my degree, she began to complain. She hated living in the wilderness and eating bugs."

"You ate bugs?"

"No, but she told her friends we did. One day I came home to find her drawers empty and a note on the kitchen table. She'd taken the camp's van and driven two days to the airport to escape. Two months later, I received the divorce papers."

"Then you became the Iron Man," she breathed. "Do you keep in touch with her?"

"No. We're both better people when we keep our pasts where they belong."

She shifted, facing him more fully, and he couldn't ignore the way the backdrop of the rain made her seem that much more fragile. And vulnerable. Oh, so vulnerable.

"You've never been seriously involved since then?"

It was hard to concentrate on the question. His attention had been captured by the way the porch light spilled a buttery warmth over her bare arms, illuminating the gooseflesh that dotted her skin.

"Christian?"

"Mmm?"

"What about serious relationships?"

"I'm all for them," he murmured, no longer able to resist the temptation this woman represented. He had to close the distance. He had to touch her.

"Christian?" His name was more of a sigh than a question. Then his arms were sliding around her waist and she stepped into his embrace with the same eagerness she'd shown that first afternoon in the Evanston motel.

Her kiss was eager and demanding as she rose on tiptoes. Christian took most of her weight, pulling her toward him so completely that he could feel her nipples rubbing against his chest and the buckle of her jeans digging into his stomach.

"Christian, we've got to stop reacting to each other like this," she whispered, breaking away and nibbling at his neck.

"Why?" he managed to gasp.

"I can't deal with this now."

"I don't think it's going to go away."

"No." Her sigh was both regretful and pleased. "But we should slow things down a bit, that's all."

He gasped as she tugged his shirt free and her hands splayed wide over his spine.

"Sure. Sure." His own fingers were working at the buttons of her blouse.

"We'll take things one day at a time."

"Okay." He barely managed to push the word from his throat as his knuckles grazed the swells of her breasts.

"It hooks in front."

He didn't need the information she supplied. He was already working at the fastener. Sliding beneath the satiny fabric, he cupped her breast and absorbed the way her body shuddered against him.

"Just for a minute," she promised. "Only for a minute." Then she was hopping against him.

He lifted her from the ground as she had silently requested, holding her fast as her legs wrapped around his hips. Moving carefully, he walked to the iron railing, settling her weight on the narrow bar. Then, his mouth was covering hers, his tongue sweeping long and deep into the sweetness beyond her lips.

The hunger that consumed him was like none he'd ever known. It raged through his body. Through his mind. His soul.

Breathing hard, he gasped for air.

"Not like this."

She shook her head, but it was obvious that she wished he hadn't spoken the words aloud.

"I can't take you like this."

"*Take* me, Christian? How very medieval."

He felt heat creep up his neck and she laughed, kissing him there, then lower and lower, until she strayed to one of his own nipples and bit him through the fabric of his shirt.

"No one 'takes' me, Christian Drake. I am master of my own body."

He framed her cheeks, forcing her to look at him. "But right now, you aren't master of your own heart."

Her eyes filled with sudden tears and she blinked them back, looking away. "Damn," she growled to no one in particular.

Christian folded her tightly against him. "When we make love, Darby—"

"When?"

With a single word, she interrupted his flow of thought, causing him to stop and think, truly think.

When they made love.

When...

Had those words really come from his mouth? Was he that sure of himself? Of her?

Tipping her face to the light, he studied what he found there. Arousal. Delight.

Acceptance.

"Yes, Darby Simms. *When* I make love to you, it will be because we both want it, because we both need it. It will be the punctuation to a happy day. The icing on some wonderful memory we both want to carry with us for the rest of our lives."

The rest of our lives.

Even though they would have parted company by then.

Christian immediately shoved that thought away. He couldn't think about the future right now. Not when the present was so damned uncertain.

"So what do we do now?" Darby asked.

He held her tight, tucking her head beneath his chin.

"Nothing. We'll move on to the next daddy candidate. In the meantime, we'll do our best to enjoy ourselves. What do you say?"

"I'd like that. I'd like that a lot."

"Promise me you won't worry about Sissy or the next prospective father."

"I—"

"Promise. It won't do any good and it will only spoil your fun."

She reluctantly nodded. "All right. I promise. After all, I can't change anything."

"That's my girl," he said in encouragement. Even so, a silent voice added, *"No, you can't change a thing by worrying. Because the future and its problems will come all too soon by themselves."*

Chapter Ten

"Is that Collin West's home?" Darby asked as she double-checked the address she'd written in her day-planner with the gilded numbers attached to the wrought-iron gates. "You're sure?" Somehow, when she'd pictured Collin West's horse-breeding ranch, she hadn't expected to find something so...so...

Opulent.

"This has to be the right place," Christian insisted.

The car idled for sometime. Not so much because either of them doubted the directions they'd been given earlier that morning when Darby had managed to get the Wests on the phone, but because of what lay ahead of them. Another candidate. Another chance to lose the little girl they'd grown to dote upon.

"What exactly *does* Eloise's diary say?" Christian asked.

"Not enough," Darby said bitterly. Then, deciding that she had to confide in him, she reached into the diaper bag and withdrew the slim, leather-bound volume, handing it to Christian. "This is all I have."

He flipped to one of the pages, which had been marked with a torn slip of colored paper. After reading the entry, he frowned and read aloud, "'November 12. Met Collin West for the first time. Had a delightful time. Talked until all hours of the morning and made arrangements for lunch in the hotel dining room. November 13. Collin had lots of advice on how I should go about marketing my paintings. Collin raises horses in Kentucky and has invited me to visit. Met *ML* and all the rest. I think they might offer me a job.'"

Christian looked up. *"ML?"*

Darby shrugged. "Your guess is as good as mine." She hesitated before saying, "But it was a woman I spoke to on the phone."

Darby had given up the pretense of being a reporter for this particular interview. When a woman had answered the phone, Darby had been so startled she'd blurted out her real name. When the voice seemed to recognize the name, Darby had been thrown even more. In the end, she'd announced that she and Christian Drake would like to drop by on their way through town if such a thing was convenient. When the stranger on the line had accepted with open alacrity, Darby had prayed that her request had not sounded as odd to the other woman's ears as it did to her own.

Especially if that woman was Collin West's wife.

Another wife?

Another opportunity for heartache?

"Are all the entries this vague?" Christian asked, and she tore her mind back to the matter at hand.

"Yes. It's more of a date book than a diary. All I've been able to determine is that she met six men within the nine-to-ten-month range of Sissy's birth—and even that information is far from scientific."

Christian handed her the book. "Well, I guess we're on to candidate number four."

Rolling into the driveway, he stopped at the imposing metal gate and punched the button to the intercom.

"Yes?" a canned voice answered from the speaker.

"It's Darby Simms and Christian Drake. We've come to—"

"Wonderful! Pull right up to the house, y'hear?"

Christian and Darby exchanged wondering glances. At the very least, it seemed that their welcome would be a warm one.

A muted buzz came from the general direction of the gate and the massive iron bars slid open on well-oiled wheels.

Christian shifted, and the car eased down a winding pea gravel drive bordered on either side with stark white fences and grazing mares. Nearly a mile from the gate, they rounded a bend shielded with trees to see the house for the first time.

Darby gasped. "It looks like something out of *Gone With the Wind,*" she whispered, studying the large white columns and floor-to-ceiling windows bordered with forest green shutters.

Christian's mouth dropped. "Tara revisited."

As if on cue, the front door opened, and a tall, middle-aged woman with dark hair and a tan riding suit rushed onto the porch. "Welcome, welcome!"

She held her arms wide.

Somewhat confused by the woman's effusive greeting, Darby unhooked Sissy from the car seat and slid outside, bumping the door shut with her hip.

"Is this the little dear?" the woman squealed, clapping her hands and reaching to take the baby from Darby's arms. "My, what a little lady you are." Then, as Christian rounded the front of the car, the woman settled the baby onto one shoulder and held out her hand.

"I'm Collin West. It's so good to meet you."

Darby blinked, her mind going suddenly blank. "*You're* Collin West?"

Collin laughed. "My, oh my, you thought I was goin' t' be a man, didn't you. Everybody thinks that. My papa wanted a boy and got me instead, so he named me Collin all the same."

Belatedly Darby shook the woman's hand, one that was undeniably feminine.

"Come on into the house. I just got back from a ride, so excuse the jodhpurs. We were all about to have juleps on the porch, so you must join us—you really *must*."

Collin preceded them to the steps and Christian took Darby's elbow. "That's Collin?" he whispered.

"It appears so."

"How does she know about the baby?"

"Your guess is as good as mine."

They were led into a foyer tiled in black-and-white squares, from there to a long hall, which led to a sunroom, and then a veranda at the back of the house.

As soon as they'd stepped outside, Collin began talking again, gesturing to the group gathered around a table set with cookies, lemonade and slender glasses filled with crushed ice and mint leaves.

"This is my husband, Mark-Lloyd."

ML?

"That tall fellow is my eldest son Brett and his wife Lilli-Sue."

Darby obediently shook hands.

"Next is Russell with my first grandchild, Ruby."

Grandchild? Collin didn't look old enough to have grown children, let alone grandchildren.

"Then there's Marla and Alana, and our youngest boy, Nick."

Darby waved to the slim teenage girls and the shy four- or five-year-old boy peeking from behind the wicker rocker.

"Grab yourselves something cool," Collin ordered, taking a seat in the rocker. "Then find a comfortable spot and help me to get caught up on all that's happened since I saw Eloise."

She lay Sissy on her lap and clapped the baby's feet together, offering the infant a host of babyish prattle along with the accompanying faces.

Darby stood numbly in one place while Christian chose a couple of the cold glasses. As she accepted the one he held in her direction, Darby felt as if she were trapped in some sort of emotional maze as she settled onto the settee. Thankfully Christian took his place beside her, his thigh pressing into hers and providing a warm anchor to reality.

"You knew Eloise well?" Darby finally asked.

Collin was still playing with the baby so her voice emerged in something of a singsong tone.

"We met about a year and a half ago when I commissioned her to complete a portrait of my children. Remind me to show it to you before you leave."

Not for the first time, Darby was struck with how much she didn't know about Eloise. How had they lost track of each other so completely in the last few years?

"She was here last November?"

"I invited her to come for Thanksgiving. That's when I discovered she was thinking of having a baby."

"Do you know what prompted her decision?"

Collin laughed. "I think it was the threat of her thirtieth birthday. One night, both of us had a bit too much rum in our toddies and she lamented about the way her eggs were getting old and she had nothing to show for them."

Collin rubbed her nose against Sissy's stomach, making the baby giggle. "How about those eggs, huh, Sissy-girl?"

Glancing up at Darby again, Collin grew sober. "It was awful the way Eloise died so suddenly. If she hadn't gone off by herself like that . . ." She regarded the baby. "At least she had a few joyful weeks with this child."

The mood grew somber and Collin cleared her throat. "Enough of that. I'm an advocate of Fitzgerald's theory that life should be enjoyed to the fullest and love should be lavished on people while they are still with us."

She regarded Darby with a secret smile. "Eloise was so fond of you. I'm glad that she decided to put Sissy in your care."

Darby opened her mouth to explain that the situation was temporary, then decided that she was tired of explaining, tired of wishing things could be different.

"She's a good baby."

"I can see that." Collin glanced from Darby to Christian. "So tell me how the two of you happened to be driving through Kentucky?"

Again, Darby silently conferred with Christian, wondering how much she should divulge. Luckily Christian decided to offer his own explanation.

Draping his arm over her shoulders, he said, "I've been out of the country for some time, working on a bridge in South America."

Collin's eyes widened. "Really? How fascinating."

"Once I returned home, I convinced Darby to join me on a vacation. I've been wanting to see more of the United States by car since I was a little boy."

"I must confess, I've always wanted to do the same," Collin admitted. "But Marc-Lloyd always refused to indulge me."

Her husband chuckled from his own rocking chair. "That's because you'd insist on driving and you make me carsick."

From that point on, the conversation flowed freely. Within minutes, Darby felt as if she'd known the Wests for years. The tension drained from her muscles and she eased even deeper into Christian's embrace, enjoying the cool breeze that smelled of grass and late summer.

It was much later, as the shadows lengthened and Collin sent Nick inside to turn on the lights that Darby forced herself to move from the comfortable nest of Christian's arms.

"We really must be going," Darby said with great reluctance as the sun began to set and a balmy peace settled over the veranda.

In all honesty, she could have lingered here forever, if it weren't for the pressing nature of her business. A call to Jean-Paul that morning had assured Darby that the designs were in production, but she still needed to get back to New York as soon as possible. Two men remained to be interviewed. One of them would have to be Sissy's father.

"You can't possibly be thinking of traveling this late at night," Collin protested. "Tell them, Marc-Lloyd."

Marc-Lloyd opened his mouth, but as was usually the case, he wasn't given the opportunity to speak.

"I won't hear of your leaving this evening—and I'll fight you tooth and nail if you don't agree to spend the weekend. That poor baby is tuckered out. Why, she needs a good night's sleep and at least a full day of rest, don't you think so, Marc-Lloyd?"

He shrugged as if to signal that he hadn't had many of his own thoughts in years.

"There, you see? You've got to stay until Monday. You simply have to."

Darby turned to Christian for help, then realized immediately that she'd be getting no aid from that direction. For the past hour, he and Marc-Lloyd had been discussing model trains as if they were a couple of kids exchanging bottle caps. Evidently, Marc-Lloyd had a whole room devoted to his hobby and he'd been urging Christian to take a look.

Too late, Darby was reminded that this was Christian's vacation and that she had been dragging him from pillar to post since the moment she'd met him. If he wanted to stay for a couple of nights and indulge in "playing conductor" with Marc-Lloyd, it would be unforgivable for her to press her own will.

"Very well," she reluctantly capitulated. "If you're sure we won't be any trouble."

"Trouble! Land sakes, no. I'll just have Jasmine fix up your quarters and put fresh sheets on the bed."

Bed.

Bed?

Ever since Indiana, they'd done their best to avoid sleeping in the same room. The fact that Collin had automatically assumed they wished the intimacy of a single bed was alarming to Darby. Her gaze skipped to Christian's and she silently pleaded for his help in defusing the situation, but he merely grinned, saying, "That would be great, Collin."

Darby considered jumping to her feet and saying, "No, no, *no!* I'm not going to share a bed with a man who—"

Who what?

Who set her nerves ablaze?

Who caused her skin to tingle whenever he entered the room?

But even as she considered such a thing, she knew it would be the height of hypocrisy. So instead of taking a stand, she did nothing. She sat in her wicker chair, staring at the man who had the ability to curl her toes from a distance.

"Jasmine!" Collin called as she swept from the veranda with the grace of her ancestors, and Darby had only to close her eyes to imagine her swathed in satin-covered crinolines as she attended to the needs of some last-minute guest for a ball.

"Good thing you gave in about staying," Marc-Lloyd murmured as his wife disappeared into the corridor.

It was the first time that Darby could remember his volunteering any information other than his talk about trains.

"She's not an easy woman when her will is crossed." His eyes sparkled in the candlelight. "Don't be surprised if she decides to throw you a barbecue."

"Oh, really," Darby said quickly. "That would really be too much trouble."

Marc-Lloyd laughed. "Not half as much trouble as it would be to talk her out of it."

"Jasmine read my thoughts and made up a room hours ago," Collin announced as she returned. "She even moved Nick's old bassinet so Sissy would have a place to sleep."

Collin gestured for them to follow her. "Come along, you two. You're both exhausted, I bet."

"Good night," Marc-Lloyd called as Darby and Christian rose and followed his wife down the back stairs.

The night was as smooth and dark as velvet as Collin led them down the back path to the small frame dwelling situated about a hundred feet away from the main house.

"This used to be Aunt Tilde's studio," Collin explained in a hushed voice as she led the way. Darby wasn't sure if the reverent tone was in deference to the sleeping baby Collin still held in her arms, or the supposed hallowedness of "Aunt Tilde."

"Aunt Tilde was a bit of an eccentric in her day," Collin explained further as she made her way up the shallow steps and fitted an old-fashioned skeleton key into the lock.

"She spent the fifties in Paris, and as far as my grandparents were concerned, the experience ruined her for decent society. When she returned, she'd cut her hair short and had taken up smoking a pipe and painting nudes. When she insisted on converting the old tack shed to some sort of Bohemian apartment, they gave her permission, but only if she agreed to keep her artistic endeavors away from the neighbors."

With that, Collin threw open the door and twisted an old-fashioned light switch. Immediately the room was flooded with a muted, buttery warmth that was tempered even more by the Tiffany lamps, which cast a kaleidoscope of color over the velvet swooning couch, the iron bedstead, and the huge mahogany armoire.

"The space isn't all that large, but it has its own bathroom—" Collin opened another door and flipped the switch to an overhead light "—as well as a tiny kitchen. The refrigerator and cupboards are stocked with goodies, so I'll leave you to your own devices for dinner. Please don't hesitate to use whatever you need. I insist that my guests choose at least one of my jars of preserves to take with them as well, so make sure you look through the supply of jars for something that appeals to your fancy.''

She set the baby inside a bassinet that had been lined with fresh sheets. Turning Sissy on her side, she propped her with a tiny pillow, then tucked Sissy's receiving blanket a little more firmly under the baby's chin.

"Sleep well," she whispered. "All of you."

Then, with what could only be described as a smug smile, she backed out of the studio, closing the door behind her.

Darby and Christian stood for some time, listening to the woman's footsteps disappearing down the path.

"She's very kind," Darby commented, needing to fill the silence.

Christian didn't answer, and when she turned, it was to discover that he was watching her with hot, brown eyes.

The room was suddenly filled with a promise of what could occur here. The passion. The lovemaking.

"You know what I'm thinking, don't you?"

Christian's low query stroked across her skin with the intensity of a caress.

"Yes." The quiet pounded around them, so rich, so full, so inescapable. "You're considering putting the icing on the cake," she murmured, repeating the phrase he'd once used with her.

Christian nodded. "But not tonight."

She could barely move, let alone say, "No. Not tonight."

"We're both too tired."

"Hmm," she added by way of an agreement.

"Plus I've had too many juleps to make it special."

Special. How could lovemaking be anything but special with this man?

"I'll take the couch," he said after several long moments, backing away...

And leaving her body thrumming with the promise of what would surely be.

Chapter Eleven

Marc-Lloyd had been correct in his assumption that Collin would insist on hosting a barbecue in their guests' honor. Darby was amazed when she, Christian and Sissy emerged from the studio to discover that a bandstand was being assembled beneath the awning of a huge striped tent, and a crew was already stringing lights over the tables and folding chairs which had been assembled on the lawn.

But Darby was given little opportunity to protest. Sissy was taken from her arms by a doting Collin, and Christian was spirited away to the train room in the basement of the antebellum house.

Darby enjoyed herself more that afternoon than she could remember doing in a long time. Soon, she and Collin were both ensconced in Collin's huge master bedroom, giggling together like school children while Darby tried on Collin's clothes in search of something to wear for the party. She didn't even argue when the bassinet was brought into Collin's room for the baby's nap. But when Collin offered to keep

Sissy there for the night to allow Darby and Christian some "private time" Darby blushed.

"That really isn't necessary," Darby insisted, sure that her hair was about to catch on fire.

"Nonsense. Every couple needs some time away from a new baby. Consider this my treat to you." Collin's eyes twinkled. "Especially since I think he'll take one look at you in my daughter's dress and haul you back to Aunt Tilde's studio."

Darby hadn't thought that her cheeks could grow any hotter, but she was mistaken. Especially when she caught sight of herself in the full-length mirror bolted to one wall of the walk-in closet. The red dress was much more daring than anything she'd ever worn before. From the front, it was a simple sheath with a modest neckline and a hem that reached to mid-thigh. But in back...

She held her breath as she peered over her shoulder at the reflection of the plunging fabric bordered with a drape of sheer silk.

"Maybe I should choose something a little less..."

"No, you don't," Collin insisted, firmly twisting Darby away from her own image. "You aren't going to change a thing. I can hear the band warming up and it is time we both found our partners."

The older woman scooped Sissy from the bassinet. The baby had also been dressed for the event in a frilly pink dress that Collin had insisted she'd bought upon hearing of Sissy's birth. The size of the dress was a little large, making the baby seem especially petite and fragile, but the baby delighted in dragging the ruffles into her mouth for a taste.

"Before we head outside, there's something I'd like to show you," Collin said as they all walked into the corridor.

She led the way to a pair of double doors in the opposite wing, disclosing a library decorated in cool whites, pastels, and mile upon mile of bookshelves.

"This is my favorite room," Collin announced as they entered. "During the winter, I positively live here."

She led Darby forward, then turned, her hand sweeping in the direction of the huge canvas hung over the fireplace. "This is the portrait that Eloise painted of my children."

It was magnificent. There was no other way to describe it. The entire painting held a warmth and an attention to detail that made it seem as if the characters being represented were flesh and blood, rather than mere two-dimensional drawings.

"*This* was painted by Eloise?"

Darby hadn't meant to sound so surprised, but she hadn't seen her friend's work since the two of them had left high school, and she was astounded by the changes she saw in Eloise's style. Gone were her stilted attempts at "modernism." Instead her portrait radiated with the passion of its creator. Not a passion for the art itself, but for the people she had studied.

"It really *is* marvelous, isn't it?" Collin said. "I think that Aunt Tilde would have approved."

She gestured to the other paintings scattered around the room, more familial studies in oils, pastels and charcoal. "All of these are hers—and they are the tamest if her collection, I assure you. As a child, I so adored these paintings of my family members, I vowed that I would find someone to immortalize my own offspring. That's why I sought out Eloise. I saw a small sketch she did of a neighbor's daughter after an equestrian match, and I knew she was just the person I wanted.''

Darby couldn't resist walking closer, touching the canvas, following Eloise's signature with her forefinger.

"I must admit that I claim responsibility for Sissy's existence," Collin added smugly.

Darby regarded her curiously.

"It was here, in this very room that I believe she made up her mind to have a baby. Eloise was finishing the last few details on the painting when Nick raced inside and slammed the door. He'd just finished his bath, and I'd put him in his pajamas, but then he'd escaped somehow. I found him here, sitting on Eloise's lap, and she was staring at him with a . . . hunger. There was no other way to describe it.''

Darby's hand slowly drifted to her side as she was caught by a facet of Eloise's nature that she'd never known before.

"I heard Nick ask her if she had a baby of her own, and she shook her head. Then she said, 'But one day, I want to have one. One day soon.'''

Collin sighed. "After that, Eloise began to ask me questions—none of them easy to answer, I can tell you. Eloise had no illusions about what it would entail to raise a child as a single parent.''

"Her father was widowed when she was very young."

"I gathered that much. I also gathered that she found her father's attention ... lacking at times."

Darby nodded. Eloise had never complained, but Darby knew that she'd never wanted to attend boarding school and that she'd resented the demands of Nashton China Works on her father's time.

"When Eloise left, I knew she planned to have a baby. I even asked her as much—quite bluntly."

Darby's lips twitched. She didn't doubt that statement at all.

"She told me she intended to take matters into her own hands right away." Collin's smile was indulgent. "And so she did." She tickled the baby under the chin. "Sissy is a lovely child. She will be like her mother one day."

Darby's throat grew tight. Yes, she would. But Darby wouldn't be the one to see her. She wouldn't be there to hold her hand when she learned to skip, or memorized the alphabet, or prepared for the prom. Sissy would be in the hands of a stranger. Someone who might love her and cherish her, or regard her as some sort of inconvenience.

Collin touched her arm and Darby started.

"I've upset you."

"No." But Darby's voice was gruff.

"Yes. I have. And I meant for this party to be a happy occasion." Collin laced her arm through Darby's. "Come along. Enough of the past. Let's see if that man of yours is ready for a dance."

That man of yours.

The very words had the ability to send a shiver of reaction through Darby's system. Not because they frightened her. Not at all. Instead they had the power to thrill her, to make her wish they were true. That they had the power to ensure a future between them.

She and Collin stepped onto the veranda in time for a slow, hip-grinding ballad to float through the air from the direction of the bandstand. It was the sort of music that slid under Darby's skin and filled her with a mysterious warmth.

Somehow, she was separated from Collin and the baby as they turned to speak to one of the guests, but she didn't mind. Automatically she found herself studying the group assembled, her gaze roaming the mill of people until it settled on a shape beneath the trees.

The shade was so thick, there wasn't really enough light for her to tell for certain that it was Christian. But she didn't need light. She was drawn to him as instinctively as a moth to a flame. He was dangerous. He was temporary. He was oh, so wrong for her at this moment in her life.

But she didn't care.

She really didn't care.

"I'll look after Sissy this evening," Collin was calling from a point somewhere behind her left shoulder, but Darby was barely listening. "You go have some fun."

Fun.

As Darby moved down the steps and soughed through the grass, the word reverberated through her head.

Fun isn't exactly what you'd use to describe what will happen next, is it? the little voice whispered, and Darby had to consciously agree. After all, "fun" was much too tame a word to describe the sensations that flowed through her veins like hot wine.

The grass was cool against her feet, the fabric of her skirt deliciously sinuous against her skin. Her body adopted a sway, a posture, that was all her own. One that declared blatantly enough to anyone who might be looking that her affections were taken. Tonight, and for some time to come.

She was only a few yards away from Christian when she was finally able to interpret his expression. What she saw there, made her heart thump against her ribs—and since the party had only begun, she couldn't claim such a reaction was due to the music, the atmosphere, the beer and the good food.

Walking to within inches of where he stood, Darby blatantly invaded his personal space, making it clear from the onset that she did not intend to play games.

She took the beer bottle he held from his lax fingers, and set it on the table beside him.

"Dance with me?"

It was more of a demand than a question. But when she took his hand and would have led him to the dance floor, he balked, tugged her back into his arms and brought her hips snugly against his. He began to sway, slowly at first, then more and more, until he dipped her over his arm and her feet automatically slid in between his own.

"Where's Sissy?" he whispered next to her ear, when they both straightened.

"Collin is watching her."

"How long?"

"Until morning."

Darby made the mistake of looking up at him, at reading the invitation shining so blatantly from his dark eyes. At that moment, she knew that—as soon as it was decently possible—the two of them would be slipping away from the dance floor. Away from the barbecue that had been organized in their honor.

And her only shame was that she would have to wait that long.

IT WAS GROWING DARK before the interest created by their visit ebbed enough for either of them to suggest leaving the party. Darby was sipping from a sweating glass of soda when Christian approached her from behind, touched her on the waist and bent next to her ear.

"Give me five minutes," he whispered.

The words alone were enough for a fire to stoke in her belly.

"Isn't that supposed to be my line?" she murmured in return.

His smile was indulgent. "Humor me."

Darby didn't know what she was supposed to do for five minutes—especially when she felt chilled the moment he stepped back.

"Five minutes," he said again as he moved away.

Knowing that she couldn't watch him leave, couldn't see the sway of those hips, and that I-don't-give-a-damn swagger he unconsciously adopted, she folded her arms beneath her aching breasts and surveyed the barbecue.

Collin was still holding court with the baby, while Marc-Lloyd and his cronies were playing horseshoes just past the braising pits.

The entire tableau should have calmed her, but it didn't. Her mind was too occupied with Christian.

Why in the world had he wanted five minutes? It wasn't as if he meant to change into some sort of exotic lingerie. She was sure that she'd seen the extent of his wardrobe already. And even if she hadn't, what did a man wear for an evening of passion? Some sort of glittery thong? A silk robe? A—

Stop it! Just stop!

She hugged her arms tighter, knowing that if she allowed herself to think of anything more, she wouldn't be able to support herself. As it was, her knees were trembling so hard, she felt as if she might collapse.

Since she didn't have a watch, she waited as long as she could. Then, when she was afraid she wouldn't be able to bear another moment, she turned and made her way into the shadows.

She followed the path through the trees, her gaze latching to the infinitesimal glow that seeped from beneath the drawn blinds.

As she approached the studio, she heard the tinny music of the windup phonograph and smiled. Music, hmm?

But not just any music. Slow jazz. Sinuous, sexy, intoxicating jazz.

Darby opened the door as noiselessly as possible, then grew still, gasping.

In the mere minutes she'd been gone, the studio had been transformed. Tiny candles had been scattered all over the room, dripping into shallow bowls and saucers.

"Christian?"

"In here."

The response came from the direction of the bathroom and she closed herself inside the studio, kicking her shoes off as she made her way to the opposite end of the room.

Somewhere inside the bathroom, the jazz melted away and the Andrews sisters began singing "Promise Me."

Promise me.

She pushed at the door and it swung noiselessly on its hinges, revealing a fantasyland of candles and lanterns that cast diamondlike patterns over the clawfoot tub that lay steaming. Waiting.

Darby gasped, stepping farther into the room. Behind her, the door closed and two hands fell over her eyes.

"Guess who?" she asked teasingly, forcing the words from a throat that had grown dry and raspy.

"I think you already know the answer to that question."

His voice had the same reaction on her nerves as velvet over bare skin.

"Don't turn around."

Immediately Darby wanted to disobey the command, but when she tried, he held her head still.

"Don't turn," he ordered again. "Promise."

She couldn't have spoken if her life depended on it.

"Promise?" he asked when she didn't respond.

Darby nodded. It was all she could manage.

He released her head, his fingers nimbly moving down the bare skin revealed by her dress.

"Where in hell did you get this thing?"

"Collin. It's her daughter's."

"Remind me to thank her in the morning." His knuckles skimmed down her spine. "Or chastise her."

"Chastise her?"

"For allowing you to torment me all evening. That dress should be declared a health hazard to the average red-blooded male."

She couldn't help but smile. A small, secret smile. The fact that she had caused this man such discomfort for the evening was more heady than any liqueur.

Christian's fingers slid beneath the straps of her dress and he eased the garment down, down, down, until it fell into a puddle of scarlet at her feet.

"You are so beautiful," he whispered, leaning so close to her that she could feel the moist warmth of his breath against her neck. Then she felt his hands whispering next to her and knew that he was removing his own shirt. His pants. Then he turned her to face him, drawing her naked body close to his.

"So beautiful," he repeated, and there was no denying the gruff edge to his voice. Instinctively she knew that his control was as limited as her own.

"You're sure?" he murmured next to her ear, and she knew that he was giving her the opportunity to stop things now, before they reached a point of no return. Physically and emotionally.

"I'm sure."

The words came from her mouth of their own volition, but she didn't regret them.

She could never regret them.

Not now.

Not ever.

Christian lifted her into his arms, carrying her to the tub and setting her into its depths. Her eyelids closed at the sheer pleasure of the water lapping against her skin. Then her lashes opened mere slits to study the man who bent over her, drizzling scented oil over her breasts.

How had she ever survived without him? she wondered as she visually caressed the sweet familiarity of his face, then lower to the width of his shoulders, the hard musculature of his chest, his stomach, and lower...

Unable to wait much longer, she took his hand, urging him into the bathtub. Water sloshed over the top, spilling in perfumed puddles across the tiled floor, but she didn't care. There was only this moment, this instant, this passion.

Then, as his lips met hers and his tongue plunged into the depths of her mouth, there was no time for thought at all. Eagerly she ran her hands over Christian's body, thrilling to the freedom she was given to explore.

She heard him groan against her, felt his body shudder in his effort to keep some modicum of control.

Smiling to herself, she leaned close to whisper, "Take me, Christian," knowing that he would remember the morning when she had brazenly announced that no man would "take" her. The fact that she would ask him to spoke volumes, relaying that she trusted him in a way that she had never trusted another living soul. Moreover, as his body settled over hers, intimately, thoroughly, she realized it wasn't just trust that she felt.

But love.

Love? How did it happen? When?

Darby's eyes squeezed closed and she clutched him to her, accepting his weight, accepting his body. And as Christian filled her with his warmth, she realized that it didn't really matter when her love had grown real.

All that mattered was that she *did* love him. Completely, utterly.

Even if such a love had no future beyond this cross-country adventure.

Chapter Twelve

The rest of the night was spent in something akin to a dream. Never before had Darby savored each minute with a man the way she did those hours with Christian. She grew to crave his touch, anticipate his pleasure and long for his kisses.

When morning dawned, sending rays of pink through the window over their bed, she regarded the advent of a new day with real regret. Once again, her responsibilities settled over her shoulders.

She would have to call New York and check on the status of the designs. Then, she would have to take the next step toward finding Sissy's father. Now, more than ever, Darby knew that she had to find answers to the mysteries that surrounded the baby in her care. Only then could Darby begin to piece together some sort of plan for the future.

Her hands shook as she buttoned her shirt. *Please, please, let those plans include Christian. Let him feel just a portion of the emotions I do for him.*

But even as the thought raced through her head, she knew her hopes were doomed. Christian had his own responsibilities. One of them being a bridge in Thailand. As much as she might wish for the two of them to have a future, any sort of a permanent relationship was impossible.

"Ready?"

She started when Christian's hands slid over her shoulders and he bent to nuzzle her neck. Immediately the strength bled from her knees and she became as weak and helpless in his arms as she had hours before when he'd brought her to the brink of pleasure.

"Yes, I'm ready," she whispered, summoning all her will in an effort to make the words emerge with some sort of coherency.

Christian's fingers tightened. "You're sure you want to head straight to Louisiana?"

She nodded, knowing that this time there was no way that she could form the words with any sense of normalcy.

Only two men remained to be questioned.

One of them had to be Sissy's father.

"Let's go, then."

Christian laced his fingers through hers, and he drew her outside to where the car had already been loaded and waited for its passengers.

As they walked, Darby was struck by how much had changed in such a short amount of time. Christian's hand lingered in the small of her back a little longer than necessary as he ushered her to the car. His fingers brushed hers as he helped to put the baby in her car seat.

"Goodbye, Collin." Darby hugged the older woman close as they said their farewells.

"I'm so glad you came to visit," Collin whispered, her own voice gruff. "Take care of yourself."

"I will."

"And Sissy."

For as long as she was able.

"And Christian."

Darby gripped the woman even tighter, suddenly overwhelmed by all of the uncertainties that lay ahead of her. There was so much that still needed to be settled, so many questions to be answered, so many decisions that would have to be faced.

Releasing Collin, she hurried to the car, double-checked Sissy's safety belt, then slid into her own place.

"Goodbye," she called one last time. "Thanks for everything."

Then they were roaring down the driveway, on their way to the next destination. The next daddy candidate.

NEW ORLEANS was like candy for grown-ups, Darby decided as the Studebaker cruised through the French Quarter, and from there to St. Charles Street.

Despite her nervousness at the reasons for their arrival in this historic city, she couldn't help but be enchanted by its charms. If only things were different, she knew she would want to linger here for several days in order to soak up the culture that surrounded her.

"Can we stop somewhere nearby? Please?" she asked eagerly. "Just for an hour or two."

Christian chuckled. "I figured we'd spend the night."

He pulled into a narrow driveway nearly obscured by a wrought-iron archway hung with ivy. As a valet rushed toward them, Christian began unhooking Sissy from the seat.

"Where are we?" Darby asked. With such elegant surroundings, she became immediately conscious of her travel-creased clothing and did her best to brush the evidence of her journey away.

"It's a little bed and breakfast my company sometimes uses to entertain clients."

Christian was already striding toward the entry and Darby hurried to catch up. "Can we get a room with such short notice?"

"We'll get a room," he said with complete certainty.

She allowed him to open the door, and as she paused to glance at the antebellum establishment with its inner courtyard, latticework railings and wide, shuttered windows, she whispered, "Don't you think it will be a bit expensive?"

"My treat," Christian murmured in return, throwing the keys to the valet and instructing him to bring all of the luggage inside.

"But—"

Christian covered her lips with his fingers as the Studebaker growled and rolled toward the converted carriage house.

"I think we deserve it, don't you?"

She wasn't sure why he thought such a thing, but she didn't argue with him. Not when the moist air from the gulf was filling her nostrils and infusing her with an effervescent energy.

"It's New Orleans, Darby," he said when she still hesitated.

New Orleans and Christian Drake. Had there ever been a more potent combination?

He led her into a lobby of pink marble and gilt, past overstuffed settees and richly carved tables. At the front desk, he conferred with the receptionist, his voice low and authoritative, but the words muffled.

As he arranged for a room, Darby stared wide-eyed at the rich draperies and thick Aubusson carpets, her heart pounding in delight at the thought of staying in such a place even for a night.

"We've got a room on the second floor," Christian informed her as he joined her near the bottom of the staircase. He was still carrying Sissy, holding her in the crook of one arm as if she were an oddly shaped football.

"They let us in?" Darby whispered as Christian's free arm swept around her waist and pulled her close.

He chuckled. "Come on. I arranged for a window with a view."

The two of them made their way to the second floor, their footsteps muffled by the woolen runner, which was held in place by shiny brass rails. Once at their destination, Christian slid a skeleton key into the lock and twisted the handle.

As soon as the door swung wide, Darby gasped, "Oh, my."

The suite was opulent—there was no other way to describe it. A huge, antique tester bed had been set on a mahogany dais, overlooking a wall of windows that looked out over the French Quarter. Beyond that, a sitting room of sorts had been made of the rest of the space. Richly upholstered divans were interspersed with huge brocade floor pillows and rugs, inviting the occupants to lie in front of the fireplace and dream.

Tiptoeing forward as if she'd entered some holy shrine, Darby peeked into the bathroom, an *ooh* of pleasure escaping her lips when she saw that it had been built to look like a Victorian solarium, complete with exotic plants and a small waterfall that emptied into a pond surrounding the whirlpool tub.

"Christian, this is decadent," she said as she turned to face him again.

"They'll bring up a portable crib for Sissy."

Her eyes widened. "Really?"

"Yeah. I . . . know one of the owners."

Immediately she was on her guard. No wonder. This wasn't the sort of place a person could walk into any night he pleased. There were probably reservations for this room every night of the year.

"Actually it belongs to my brother and his wife."

"Your brother?" she echoed weakly. Damn.

Damn, damn, damn.

She wasn't ready to encounter real life.

Not yet.

"Yeah. I thought they should meet you."

The words shimmered in the air, carrying with them their own charged effect.

"Why?"

Christian shifted slightly, tucking his fingers into his pockets in a way she found completely endearing.

"Isn't that supposed to be what you do when you're serious about someone?"

Serious.

Serious?

"Is that what we are?" she asked somewhat breathlessly, feeling her whole body begin to tremble with anticipation.

"Yeah. I think so. Don't you?"

She hesitated before saying, "But our time together is limited?"

She'd been the first person to voice the unspoken obstacle. Christian's expression grew grave, but she forced herself to continue. "As much as I wish things could be different, Christian, I have to get back to New York."

His head dipped and he stared at the floor as if the pattern of the carpet held the secrets of the world. "And I will soon be off to Thailand."

Darby didn't realize she'd been holding her breath, waiting for him to offer some alternative arrangement. But there was no way to avoid the truth. They would eventually have to part.

"I would still like to introduce you to my brother and his wife," Christian said, lifting his chin and piercing her with a glance.

She couldn't have prevented her tremulous smile. "I would like to meet them, too."

"Good. They'd like to go to dinner with us. My niece Becca is fourteen and she's volunteered to watch the baby."

"That would be great."

"Jan, my sister-in-law, is really nice. I think the two of you will get along right away. But Brigham..."

"Your brother?" she clarified.

"Yes. He might give you a hard time."

Darby's heart lurched in a telling manner. "Why?"

"I've never made a point of bringing someone to meet them before."

The fact that she had been the first woman for which he'd done such a thing warmed her heart.

"What about Sissy?" she asked nervously, wondering how Jan and Brigham would interpret Christian's dating a woman with an infant. "How are you going to explain—"

"They have cable," he said before she could finish. "They've been avid followers of 'The Gossip Exchange' since they first saw my picture."

She sank onto an upholstered chair. "Oh, no."

Christian waved aside her fears. "Don't worry. I told them that Sissy is your ward for the time being, and that the news reports of our meeting were highly exaggerated."

"Did they believe you?"

"Sure. Especially when I told them you kidnapped me at gunpoint."

She gasped, jumping to her feet, then realized he was teasing.

He cupped her face in his hands, forcing her to meet his gaze. In it, she saw such richness, such adoration, that she could barely breathe.

"Come on," he murmured enticingly. "Let's hit the town for a few hours, maybe find something special to wear. Then we'll meet Jan and Brigham at Mr. B's.''

Darby was tempted, so very tempted. But she couldn't ignore the fact that they had hurried to New Orleans for a reason. Now that they were here, she couldn't put off the intent of their original errand.

She shook her head. ''No.''

Christian's disappointment was evident. ''Why not?''

She gripped his wrists, drawing upon the obvious strength she found there. ''I've got to arrange a meeting with Lucien DuBois.''

Christian studied her carefully, but didn't try to talk her out of it. For that she was glad. If he'd suggested they run away and refuse to think of the consequences, she would have been sorely tempted to do so.

But even as she thought of such a thing, she knew that Christian would never belittle this quest she'd assigned herself.

''Fine. See if you can reach Mr. DuBois by phone. Have him meet us at Mr. B's within the hour. We'll take Sissy with us, just in case.''

Just in case.

Just in case the man demanded a look at his daughter.

''What if. . .'' She couldn't finish the sentence and Christian evidently understood. Folding her close, he rocked her as if she were no more than an infant herself.

''Shh. We'll take things one minute at a time. I don't think my family would mind if we put the plans on hold. If, after the meeting, you're up to a night on the town, my niece can come with her folks and take the baby back home by taxi. Okay?''

"Thank you," Darby whispered.

"Hey," he said, cajoling her out of her somber mood. "There's a fifty-fifty chance he isn't the father, either.''

Darby hugged him close, pressing herself against his hard chest, his warmth, his security.

Fifty-fifty.

She still didn't like the odds.

CHRISTIAN SAT at the table he'd been given by the maître d' at Mr. B's and propped Sissy in his lap. Staring at the woman who waited across the room, he wondered why the Fates had such a twisted sense of humor. Weeks ago, he'd been contemplating this road trip as a form of relaxation, or centering himself, of reevaluating his goals. But since meeting up with Darby, he hadn't thought of his own life at all. He'd become embroiled in helping her cope with an infant who needed a father, and he'd forgotten his own petty concerns. Unfortunately, in immersing himself in their world, he'd been given a taste of what he'd been missing for some time.

A woman who entranced him.

A child who needed him.

Pulling Sissy more securely against his chest, he admitted to himself that he wasn't looking forward to the next few minutes. If that DuBois character turned out to be Sissy's father, Christian knew he might just deck the man. How dare he abandon a lover who could be pregnant? How dare he not know that Sissy had been conceived?

But even as the thought raced through Christian's mind, he was faced with an even more startling fact. What if Darby were pregnant? Granted, they'd taken precautions nearly every time they'd made love.

Nearly.

That's how babies are made, pal.

Christian took a deep breath, held it, then exhaled when he realized the fact didn't terrorize him as much as it had when Rachael had informed him she was pregnant. At eighteen, he hadn't been ready to be a father. Now...

Sissy shifted her head so that she could gnaw at his thumb, and Christian stared down at her, his heart pounding as if he'd run a mile.

He wanted a daughter, he realized suddenly. He wanted a baby like this one.

He wanted a wife.

His gaze bobbed to Darby, noting how the recessed lighting shot her hair with highlights and made her skin seem as soft as a rose petal.

You can't have her, the voice inside him warned.

She couldn't come with him to Thailand. She had her own career waiting for her in New York. And as much as she worried about Ricardo Yvonne's precious designs, he knew she loved her job. One day, he was certain that she would become a designer of her own line—and he didn't doubt she would be successful. She was very passionate about her work.

She was passionate about a good many things.

Including Christian Drake.

So what was he going to do?

Christian sighed, reaching for the lime and soda on the table. He wished he had more time to sort out an answer to all his questions. If he hadn't committed to the job in Thailand, he could have spent a few more months in the States. As it was, he was tied down by his own commitments.

But as his thumb became soaked with drool and the baby continued to gum his knuckle like a newborn lamb, he couldn't deny that he wished things could be different. Very different indeed.

DARBY RAN HER FINGERS up and down the stem of her wineglass, her stomach tightening into knots. Time and time again, she looked up at Christian who sat at a table on the opposite end of the room. She kept studying the baby cradled in his arms, and each time, she wished that things could be different. If only Eloise hadn't demanded she find Sissy's father. If only Darby could keep the baby.

Keep Christian.

The thought seared through her heart with the strength of a lightning bolt, and she found it all but impossible to push away. She was insane to even entertain such a fantasy, but she couldn't help envisioning how her life would be, a cottage surrounded by a picket fence, a yard with a swing, a husband who built bridges.

Bridges in faraway countries with exotic names.

She shook her head to clear it. No. She mustn't think about such things. If she did, she would have to drop to the ground and bawl.

"Excuse me, Miss Simms?"

Glancing up, she found a tall, elegant man standing by her table.

"Is something wrong?" he asked, his brows furrowing over incredibly dark green eyes.

"Wrong?" Darby echoed.

"You're crying."

Her hands shot to her face, and she gasped when she encountered the wetness of her own tears.

The man sank into the chair beside her, pulling a snowy white handkerchief from the pocket of his raincoat. "Here."

She took it with some hesitance, but since she had no other recourse than the restaurant napkin, she swiped her cheeks.

"You're very kind."

"Not at all. I've often longed for the opportunity to do that. I've carried white handkerchiefs for years, yet, never once have I been able to offer it to a beautiful lady in distress."

Darby felt herself flush and looked at Christian.

He was scowling.

"Lucien DuBois, I presume," she murmured, finally realizing that the maitre d' must have sent him to her table.

"Guilty as charged."

He grinned, flashing even white teeth—and in that instant, Darby knew why her friend had fallen for this man. He exuded an aura of sensitivity and masculinity.

Darby offered a soft laugh, still wiping beneath her eyes and praying her mascara hadn't begun to run. "You must think me a perfect fool."

"Not at all. A woman's entitled to her emotions, no matter where they might strike her." His grin widened even more.

Somewhat muddled by his smile, his manner, she reached for her glass, then paused. She had been so prepared for an adversary—or at the very least, a disgruntled playboy—she found herself disarmed by this man's ability to make her feel immediately at ease.

"I'm sorry, you must think I'm incredibly rude," she began, nudging the leather-bound menu in his direction. "Can I order you a drink? Something to eat?"

He shook his head, plunging his hands into the deep pockets of his coat and slouching in the chair with elegant ease. "No. But thank you all the same. I have a basketball game in an hour with the kids and if I'm not in top form, they run me ragged."

Her brows lifted. "Basketball?"

"I coach a youth group."

He coaches a youth group.

"You like children, then?"

"Very much."

Darby was inundated with relief, even as she felt a shiver of dismay. This was the man. This was Sissy's father. She knew it deep in her bones. He was everything that Eloise had ever dreamed of encountering in a man. Easy sophistication, sensitivity, good looks.

Her hands began to tremble.

"So you wanted to talk to me about Eloise," Lucien prompted when the silence fell between them.

"Yes." The word was little more than a croak.

"She was a delightful woman. She and I spent many hours at the church talking."

"Church?"

"She'd come to the cathedral to study one of the stained-glass windows, which is being repaired. Since I was helping to oversee the restoration work, we saw a good deal of each other."

No doubt.

"You became good friends," Darby said.

It wasn't a question, but he answered it nonetheless. "Yes. She was a delightful woman. I was very troubled to hear about her death. When I met her, she was very vulnerable."

This was the first time that Darby had heard that particular word used in conjunction with her friend.

"She was feeling very blue, very lonely," he continued.

"Oh, really? Why?"

He didn't immediately answer. "Suppose you tell me who *you* are, Darby. Then, I'll see about answering your questions."

She opened her mouth to insist she was a reporter doing a story, then changed her mind. Of all the men she'd met, all the men she'd investigated, this one seemed the most inclined to deal with the truth in a positive manner.

"When Eloise died, her will named me as executor of her estate."

"Ahh," Lucien drawled. "So all this has something to do with her worldly possessions." He sighed, staring into the shadows of the room as if pondering that thought. "Am I to assume, then, that I was mentioned in the document as well?"

"In . . . a matter of speaking," Darby hedged.

His green eyes met hers.

"Lucien, I'm not sure how much you knew about Eloise's background, but she came from an extremely wealthy family."

He nodded and it was obvious that such a fact was not new to him.

Encouraged by his reaction, Darby said, "Since then, a good many people have tried to claim her fortune."

His eyes closed briefly as if the very fact pained him. "I can understand how that would happen, but rest assured that you won't receive any such demands from me. If I have been mentioned in her will, I will deny any such claims."

"But—"

"No, I insist. Eloise used me as a sounding board, that's all. I think the fact that she wasn't Catholic, made me seem quite safe and anonymous. I was the perfect listener, but little more."

Little more? He'd been her lover. He'd fathered her child.

"But I've promised to see that her wishes are fulfilled."

"Then give any inheritance she gave me to charity."

Darby leaned forward, wondering why she was having such a hard time communicating the truth to this man. "I think you misunderstand me. The matter is a little more complicated than that." She signaled to Christian. "Eloise didn't ask me to give her money away. All of that has been held in trust for Sissy."

Lucien's brows rose. "Sissy?"

Christian was standing by the table now, the baby in his arms. Sissy must have known she was about to become the center of attention because she grinned, showing toothless gums and chubby cheeks.

"Lucien, this is Eloise's daughter."

Lucien twisted, and rather than appearing shocked or even dismayed, a wide, astonished smile tipped his lips.

"A daughter! How wonderful!"

He stood then, leaning toward the baby and tickling her under the chin. "A baby! She had hoped to begin a family, to give her life some sense of purpose and stability." He sobered. "I'm glad she was able to realize at least a portion of her dreams before she died. I prayed that I'd been able to offer her some sort of help."

Darby shifted, wishing she could deny the inevitable, that this man was Sissy's father. Christian was scowling, obviously suspicious of the competition for the infant's affections, but Darby knew she'd found her man. And if she had to give Sissy away, at least it was to someone like this.

"May I hold her?" Lucien asked.

Darby dipped her head in acknowledgment.

Lucien shrugged out of his raincoat and draped it over the back of the chair. As he reached out to take the girl, Darby's gaze ran over his form, memorizing this moment for the future when she herself was feeling vulnerable and lonely. At such times, she would envision Lucien's dark waving hair, black eyes, square jaw, ebony suit, white collar and—

White collar.

A strip of a white collar.

A priest's collar.

A *priest*.

"Father?" she croaked.

Lucien responded immediately, "Yes?"

"Father, how long have you been a priest?"

"About ten years. Why?"

Darby looked at Christian, who was suddenly much more jovial toward the man.

"You and Eloise never . . . I mean you weren't . . ."

He looked at her blankly. "We weren't what?"

Darby shifted uncomfortably. How did one ask a priest if he'd ever broken his vow of chastity?

"I think what Darby wants to say is that you and the baby have similar coloring."

"You think so?" Lucien held the infant up, peering at her more closely. "Too bad there's no chance of that, is there?" His eyes twinkled as he met Darby's gaze. "That is what you wanted to ask, isn't it?"

Darby felt a scalding tide of heat seep into her cheeks, and Father DuBois's chuckle deepened in delight. "Don't look so shocked, my dear. I work with the kids on the streets, and they keep me well-grounded in reality. No, this little tyke isn't mine, and that's the truth, plain and simple."

He spent a few more minutes cuddling the baby and conversing with her in French. Then, after a quick check of his watch, he reluctantly handed her to Darby.

"I wish that I could spend more time with all of you. I really would like the opportunity to hear more about the little one." He sighed. "But I fear that some of my own 'children' are waiting for me—good kids who manage to stay clean and sober by beating the socks off me and a few of the sisters from Holy Cross Hospital at least once a week."

After offering the baby one last caress, he pointed a finger at Darby. "I expect a Christmas card or a letter now and then, understand? She may not be mine in body, but I would still like to consider her a close friend of the spirit. Let me see her grow."

Then he gathered his raincoat, offered one last wave and was gone.

Darby sank into her chair, stunned. Five men. Five men eliminated from their candidacy as Sissy's father.

"You could call the parish just to make sure he's a real priest," Christian suggested. "He might be lying to get out of a paternity suit."

Darby glared at Christian. "I hardly think that's necessary."

"I'm just trying to be thorough." But it was clear by the sparkling amusement in his own eyes that he was only joking. Humming to himself, he picked up the menu that Father DuBois had never bothered to read. "So... What's for dinner?"

"This isn't funny, Christian."

His expression was openly mischievous. "It isn't?"

"No! I nearly accused a... a *priest* of... of..."

"Philandering?"

"Shh!"

He laughed even harder. "I don't know why you have your knickers in a knot. You should feel relieved."

"Why?"

"Because he isn't the one. He isn't Sissy's father."

At that moment they were both struck by the same realization and even Christian's euphoria ebbed.

"That means that Compton Smythe is," Darby whispered.

He took a deep breath. "You're sure?"

"There were no other names mentioned in Eloise's diary."

"A diary that we both agree is incredibly vague."

"It may be vague, but I think Eloise would have noted the father of her baby, don't you?"

He didn't answer and they both lapsed into a morose silence.

"What if I offered you an alternative?" Christian asked sometime later.

She rubbed at the ache gathering between her brows. "What sort of alternative?"

"What if I volunteered to marry you?"

Darby stared at him, her heart flip-flopping in her chest. "What did you say?" she whispered.

"I could marry you. If you had a husband, maybe you could sue for guardianship."

She stared at him, trying to discern his motives. Was it only the baby that had spurred such an offer? Could she dare to hope that there was something more? Something that he was hesitant to add because both of them had been reticent about voicing the emotions that were still so fragile between them.

But as much as she wanted to ask him more, she didn't.

She couldn't.

"So this is the famous Darby Simms," a tall, slender man said from behind Christian's shoulder. As her gaze slid up the stranger's frame, one so much like Christian's, she knew immediately that she was about to meet his brother and his wife.

Please, please, let me make a good impression, she whispered in silent prayer.

But even that thought was drowned out by an even more insistent plea.

Please, please, don't let Christian's offer be a joke.

"DID THEY LIKE ME?" she asked Christian much later after they'd made love in the huge tester bed and he'd folded her close to his side.

"They loved you."

"How can you tell?"

"Brigham teased you."

"You told me he'd tease me."

"But only if he liked you. Otherwise, he would have been polite."

She ducked her face into his shoulder, hiding the grin she couldn't contain. Since Brigham had spent the whole night treating her like some sort of kid sister, she supposed she'd passed the test.

"I'm glad I didn't disappoint you."

Christian ran his hand down her spine. "You could never disappoint me."

Silence spooled around them, warm and quiet and rich. Then, Christian said, "You haven't answered my question."

"Which question?"

"Marriage."

She squeezed her eyes closed, knowing that as much as she might be tempted to accept his offer, she couldn't. If this relationship was ever to reach its full potential, it must be treated with utmost care. She couldn't rush into a commitment when neither of them were sure of what they wanted.

"No."

She felt his muscles stiffen. Odd. Shouldn't he be growing more relaxed?

"It wouldn't be right, Christian."

"Why?"

She pulled away from him, sitting at the edge of the bed, her feet hanging over the edge, not quite touching the ground.

"Marriage is a serious business. I can't become your wife just to give Sissy a home."

She felt him sit up behind her. "You were about to marry Chauncey Fitch for about the same reason."

"Which is why I've learned my lesson." She whirled, clutching his hands. "Please don't press me about this. I've learned a lot these past few weeks. I appreciate everything you've done for me. But I couldn't ask you to marry me for Sissy's sake. You deserve more.'' She touched his cheek. "We both deserve more.''

He was so still, she feared she'd offended him. Then at long last, he lay down, pulling her with him. Snuggling against his side, she squeezed her eyes shut, wishing that she had the courage to tell him the rest. That she loved him. That she would do anything to see their relationship develop into a mutual future.

But she couldn't.

Instead she said, ''Can we head toward Virginia as soon as possible?''

His hands drew her closer against him and she fought the tightness gripping her throat.

''Sure.''

Then they both lapsed into silence. A silence that preceded quick caresses, then feverish lovemaking.

As if they both knew that time was their enemy and all three of them would soon have to part.

Chapter Thirteen

Compton Smythe Research Facility.

Darby regarded the brass sign bolted to the large, box-shaped, concrete building and shivered, clutching the baby a little tighter in her arms.

It had been foolish, she knew, but while she and Christian had been driving north from Louisiana, she'd begun to fabricate possible scenarios in her mind. She'd imagined the man she would meet, the interest the baby would receive, the warm welcome that would ensue.

But now, staring up at the cold, dun-colored clinic, she wondered if any of that would occur, or if Sissy would merely be wrenched from her arms and the door shut in Darby's face.

Darby sighed. She shouldn't have allowed herself to think of this moment at all. That way she wouldn't feel such a keen disappointment at what she'd seen so far. She wasn't sure what she'd expected. Maybe a warm brick edifice, lots of ivy, historic charm. Instead it appeared she was about to enter a New Age war bunker.

"You don't have to do this, Darby. I can drive away and you can claim you never found the father."

She knew Christian was right. No one would fault her if she balked at this last hurdle. She could say she'd done everything possible. She could even insist that the lawyers handle this last inquiry.

But her love for Eloise and Sissy Nashton would not allow it. Neither would her conscience.

"Let's go, Sissy."

She stepped away from the Studebaker, knowing that Christian still wanted to join her. But as soon as they'd entered Virginia and located the address to the clinic in the phone directory, she'd insisted that this was something she needed to do on her own.

Darby's steps were crisp and efficient as they led her forward, despite the fact that her knees felt as if they were the consistency of Jell-O. She even managed to summon a little smile when she saw her own grim expression reflected in the mirrorlike windows of the clinic.

"No matter what happens, Sissy," she murmured to the baby in her arms. "I love you. That will never change. Never."

The automatic doors opened with a muted *whoosh*. Pausing infinitesimally, Darby took in the decor of the lobby. Green and black ceramic tiles had been laid geometrically over the floors. Plush leather couches had been arranged around marble and glass tables, which held enormous bouquets of waxy looking tropical flowers. The whole effect managed to be both elegant and aloof.

A few yards away, an octagonal reception desk gleamed beneath a wealth of hidden lighting, revealing a single phone and an elegantly attired woman.

Darby wanted to turn and run, especially when the woman regarded her with lifted brows. There was something about the too-clean desk and too-beautiful woman that caused gooseflesh to rush over Darby's skin. But her feet carried her forward, her heels echoing hollowly on the tiles.

"May I help you?" Miss Too-Beautiful inquired.

Darby's throat had grown so dry, she feared anything she said would emerge in a croak.

"I'd like..."

Not a croak, a squeak.

She cleared her throat. "I need to see Dr. Smythe, please."

The receptionist's carefully penciled brows rose even further.

"I beg your pardon?"

"I'd like to see Dr. Smythe."

Too-Beautiful frowned. "Do you have an appointment?"

"No. But I've come a very long way to see him and it's very important."

The woman shook her head. "I'm afraid that's impossible." Her eyes flicked to the baby and back again. "Dr. Smythe does not see his... guests."

Darby's brows creased. "Guests?"

The woman's eyes roamed warily around the lobby as if she were being observed by some sort of hidden camera. "*You* know what I mean," she murmured under her breath.

Darby wanted to punch the woman in the middle of her too perfect nose. "No, I'm afraid I don't."

The receptionist leaned forward to whisper, "The doctor never, *ever* meets with his...customers. All of his work is done in the lab. Dr. Compton does all the screening."

Darby's knees threatened to buckle altogether. "Dr. Compton?" she whispered. "There's two of them?"

The receptionist blinked at her in surprise. "Of course. That's how this facility received its name."

Darby was shaking so hard now, she could hardly stand, and the receptionist evidently noted the fact.

"Oh, my gosh," she murmured, her facade of perfection faltering and revealing her for the teenager she really was. "Don't faint on me, okay? Oh, my gosh. Oh, my gosh!"

She pressed a button on her console. "Emily, come here. Quick!"

A door that had been hidden in the wall slid open and a gray-haired woman emerged. She took one look at Darby and motioned to the girl.

"Bring her in here, Addy."

Darby was led into an employee lounge of some sort and was urged into a seat.

"Get her some coffee."

Emily took the baby from Darby's arms, handling the infant like the veteran grandmother her gray hair, support hose and reading glasses made her appear to be.

"Put your head between your legs," she ordered. "You're looking awfully pale."

Darby did as she was told, taking gulps of air so that the haziness receded. When it did, she was confronted with the horrible reality. Two men. Compton Smythe was two men.

Her breath came quick and hard, dissolving into gulps, then sobs.

The two women stared at her as if she'd lost her mind, but she couldn't help it. All the miles, all the trouble, all the worries, and she still had *two* men she had to screen, not one.

Emily juggled the baby into the crook of one arm and used her free hand to pat Darby on the back. "There, there, miss..."

"Darby. Darby Simms."

"There, there. Whatever is the matter? You have a beautiful baby."

At that pronouncement, the sobs came quick and hard, and tears flooded down Darby's cheeks. "You don't understand," she wailed. "She's not m-mine...I want Sissy to be...mine, more than you'll ever know!"

Darby knew she'd lost what little control she'd ever had on her emotions, but she couldn't seem to stop herself.

The women pulled two chairs close and their wide interested eyes were all Darby needed to urge a confession.

"Eloise was my best friend—my best friend ever! But I...I didn't even k-know she w-was pregnant." The last word was all but a keening moan, and Addy reached for a box of tissues, extending them in Darby's direction.

After wiping her eyes, Darby continued. "When s-she died, Eloise t-told me to take the baby t-to the f-f-father. But she never bothered to tell me *who* that was...s-so I've been traveling cross-country with a man I met b-because of a flat tire—a *flat tire,* for heaven's sake!—in order to find him."

"Who?" Addy asked.

"The f-father."

"The baby's father?" Addy whispered, peering at Emily in confusion.

"Of course, the baby's father," Emily grumbled, patting Darby's hand. "Keep up with the facts, Addy. The father is the man with the flat tire."

Darby shook her head. "No, that's Christian."

"Christian?" Both women echoed at once.

"You see, I was almost ready to marry one of them," Darby supplied.

"One of what?" Now, even Emily seemed confused.

"The fathers."

The two women frowned, but Darby was too upset to backtrack and explain.

"His name was Chauncey." She rushed on. "H-he offered me a marriage of convenience, but just before I walked down the aisle, I discovered he'd had m-mumps as a ch-child and he was sterile."

When she looked to the women for confirmation of the horror she'd felt, they nodded sympathetically, but didn't speak.

"Obviously I was shocked!"

"Of course you were," Emily soothed, patting her hand. "Addy, maybe you'd better get us all some coffee."

The girl rushed to obey.

"I couldn't possibly go through with a marriage based on lies and thievery," Darby said, taking up her monologue when Addy returned. "He only wanted Sissy's money! The Nashton fortune."

The women glanced at the baby.

"She's worth over a million, you know."

Addy's eyes widened and she gasped, pointing an excited finger in Darby's direction. "*You're* the woman on that gossip show, aren't you? The friend of Eloise Nashton who died in a Swiss avalanche."

Darby nodded miserably. "When I ran out of the church, I discovered I didn't have a way to leave. Christian was there, changing a flat tire, and I jumped into his car. I all but *hijacked* the man and told him to take me to Tahoe. When I got sick on his junk food, he took care of Sissy—and soon I found I didn't want to leave him at all."

A sob welled from her chest at the memories. Those wonderful, wonderful memories. "He's been so good to me. He's driven us both cross-country. Sissy adores him as much as I do.''

"Naturally," Emily said, tickling the baby beneath the chin. "Good taste in men starts at an early age.''

"Exactly!" Darby exclaimed, glad that these women were finally grasping what it was so hard for her to express in words. "That's why I wanted to accept his offer.''

"What offer?" Addy breathed.

"He proposed to me.''

Addy beamed. "You accepted, of course.''

"No.''

"Why not?''

"I couldn't marry him like that." Her chin wobbled uncontrollably. "I love him too much to tie him down—and I can't give up my job. Even if I wanted to, they need me for at least six months.''

Addy's brows creased. "But—''

"Hush, Addy," Emily scolded. "Let her talk.''

"If I'd married him, he said we could sue for custody and become a real family. All three of us.''

Emily made a clucking sound in her throat. "But you couldn't do that. Not when you'd promised to take the baby to her father.''

"Yes!" Finally, someone understood her predicament. "But the second man I investigated wasn't the right one, either. He'd had a vasectomy. The third turned out to have only one—" she flicked a glance at her lap "—you know.''

"Ohhhh," the women echoed wisely.

"Plus, he'd been busy with his wife and new babies whenever he wasn't on the race circuit."

Emily's brows rose. "Are you talking about the DaVincis?"

"Yes!"

"Lovely people."

"You know them?" Darby asked in confusion.

"Yes, of course."

This time it was Darby's turn to be confused. "But how?"

"Never mind, dear. Go on with your story."

"Well, the fourth candidate ended up to be a woman."

Addy choked on her own coffee.

"What I meant was that, of the six names I investigated, I mistakenly assumed one was a man when, in fact, it was a woman."

It was clear her audience didn't completely understand, but she plunged on nonetheless.

"The fifth man was a father—I mean, not a father as in having children, but a *Father,* as in a priest."

Emily's and Addy's eyes widened.

"Naturally he wasn't the *baby's* father."

"Naturally," they both said at once.

"So that led me here, to this research facility. I was so sure that Dr. Compton Smythe was her father and that this whole awful mess would be finished." Darby's voice was growing choked again. "But now I've discovered that there are *two* of them, and I don't think I can bear to do this—she should be mine, don't you see? She should be *mine.*"

Her declaration dissolved into a fresh round of crying and Emily turned to Addy.

"Call Dr. Compton and Dr. Smythe. Send them down here immediately."

"But—"

"Tell them it's an emergency."

"Yes, ma'am."

"Then I want you to go to Records."

"But I'm not allowed to—"

"I don't care what you're allowed to do. I want you to do a search for Eloise Nashton on the computer and if you find a file, bring a hard copy to me. I think there might be a simple solution to this dilemma."

"But—"

"Go!"

Addy stood and rushed from the room.

Darby did her best to calm down, knowing that one way or another, she was about to have her answers.

By the time the door opened again, she was quiet, if still shaking to the core and prone to the odd tears that gathered in her eyes. Taking Sissy from Emily's arms, she steeled herself for what was to come.

"The doctors are on their way," Addy whispered as she entered, carrying a sheaf of computer print-outs. "Here's the file."

Emily balanced her glasses on her nose and began to examine the documents, just as an elderly couple entered the lounge. One male. One female.

Darby bit her lip. If these were the doctors Compton and Smythe, then at least one of them had been ruled out.

She studied the stooped, white-haired man. He was so small and wizened. With a little luck, he might be in his seventies, but was more likely in his eighties or beyond.

"Dr. Smythe!" Emily shouted as if the man were hard of hearing. "This is one of your babies!"

The old man perked up, then turned to look at Sissy.

Darby stiffened, automatically shielding the infant from his gaze, but the doctor toddled forward, holding out his hands and saying, "May I?"

Since the baby was his, so obviously his, Darby relinquished the girl, a sick heaviness invading her heart. What kind of future did Sissy have with a father who could die before she reached puberty?

"Look, Martha," Smythe said, taking Sissy with gentle, practiced hands. "It's a girl. A beautiful girl."

The woman cooed and stroked the baby's cheek.

"It seems there's been some confusion over this baby, Dr. Compton, Dr. Smythe," Emily said, her voice still loud enough to carry.

"Oh, really?" Dr. Smythe appeared to be giving his colleague only a fraction of his attention. Most of his energies centered around Sissy.

"The baby's mother has died."

That caught both of the doctors unawares and they stared at Emily.

"She instructed this woman, the baby's guardian, to find the birth father."

Dr. Compton and Dr. Smythe both studied Darby, obviously concerned.

"Oh, dear," Dr. Compton murmured.

"I have Ms. Nashton's file here," Emily continued, "and I wondered if you would give me permission to bend the rules. If so, I'll give Ms. Simms a little more information on the father—without disturbing his privacy, of course."

Darby's fingers curled around the arms of her chair. "I don't understand. I thought that Dr. Smythe..."

Dr. Smythe chortled. "No, no. I'm not the baby's father."

"You see, Darby," Emily inserted before Darby could speak. "This isn't just *any* research facility. It's a fertility clinic specializing in artificial and in vitro fertilization."

Darby's heart began a slow, sluggish beat.

"Artificial insemination?"

In a flash, she remembered all she'd learned about Eloise from her cross-country search.

If Darby were to piece together the information from the road trip and the chronological order of the diaries, she would bet that Eloise had first visited Collin West and had fallen in love with the woman's children. Once the idea had been planted, she had gone to Louisiana, where Father DuBois had helped her to sort out her feelings and come to a decision to raise a child alone.

Next, she probably ran into Chauncey, who could charm the stars from the skies. It would have been so easy for Eloise to consider such a man as a candidate for her child's father. But somehow, Chauncey must have revealed his true self. A man who was actually selfish, manipulative, and sterile.

If Darby were to bet what happened next, she would put her money on Nick Rassmussen being the second possible candidate. She must have entered into a relationship, knowing that she hoped a baby would result from the experience, only to discover the man had undergone a vasectomy.

Sometime soon after, she must have met Alec and Sally DaVinci. From them she had learned about Compton Smythe. All along, Darby had assumed the names belonged to a single man. But the pages of Eloise's diary had been cryptic and uninformative. Only now did she know that Compton Smythe wasn't a person, but a place.

A clinic specializing in artificial insemination.

Emily was riffling through the pages, and the noise drew Darby out of her haze.

"Eloise Nashton came to us a little over a year ago," Emily began, reading from the sheets. "She completed all the necessary tests, physicals, and screening activities. At that time, she was given a catalog of profiles outlining the physical and educational backgrounds of our donors. She chose number 427-601A, a white male of French ancestry."

French. As in Paris, the Left Bank, an artist's Mecca.

"At the time of his donation, he was a guest lecturer at Columbia University, thirty-seven years old, with a master's degree in architectural history. The profile further explained that he was fluent in three languages, loved horses and wine and opera.''

Opera. Eloise adored the opera.

"He was in excellent physical condition, with dark hair, blue eyes and an above average IQ. Conception was successful on the second attempt." Emily closed the file and placed it on her lap. "I'm afraid that's all I can tell you, other than the fact that the donor signed a legal release, dissolving all ties to any future children his sperm might create."

Dr. Smythe gently laid Sissy in Darby's arms and Darby held the baby as a matter of reflex.

"I'm afraid she will not be reunited with her biological father," the old man said. "It isn't possible."

Dr. Compton touched Darby's shoulder. "The woman specified in her will that you should find the father?"

Darby nodded. "Yes. She drafted the document will just after giving birth."

"Ahh." Compton's eyes twinkled. "I take it she was medicated?"

"Yes, it made her rather loopy for..." Darby's words trailed away. "How did you know?"

Compton shrugged. "It happens. The euphoria, the exhaustion, the medication. We've had letters from postpartum mothers requesting this sort of thing before. After they grow more lucid, they remember that they've signed a waiver that refuses them the right to the donor's identity."

Darby stared at Compton, then Smythe, stunned by what she was hearing.

Sissy's father had been a test tube filled with anonymous sperm.

A test tube.

Bit by bit, her muscles were released from their inactivity and her mind began to function more clearly. As it did, she was confronted by one overwhelming fact. Darby had been sent on a wild-goose chase by a woman under the influence of painkillers. Eloise had probably never *really* intended for Darby to find Sissy's father. If she hadn't been killed so suddenly, she would most likely have drafted a new document. One that would have been much more complete and much more logical.

"Were any arrangements made in Eloise's will should the father not be found?" Compton asked, bringing Darby's attention screaming back to the matter at hand.

"I don't know," Darby murmured, numb with all that had occurred. "I'll have to call the lawyers."

Smythe gestured to the phone. "Dial nine for an outside line." He made a shooing gesture to the other members of the clinic. "Let's give her some privacy."

Darby waited until they had all left before taking a deep breath and reaching for the phone. Her hands trembled as she dialed the number she'd learned by heart.

"Dalton, Dalton, and Crumm."

"Hi, Maxine? It's Darby. Can I talk to Bill, please?"

CHRISTIAN BEGAN HIS WAIT in the car. For the first few minutes he was still, thoughtful, somber. By the time half an hour had passed, he was tapping the wheel with his thumbs. Thirty minutes after that, he'd abandoned the car altogether and was pacing the flagstones in front of the building.

Dammit! Why couldn't this bizarre story have a happy ending? Why couldn't he and Darby and the baby become a family?

A family.

A real family.

The idea caught his brain and couldn't be dislodged. Granted, they would be an unusual group. Ordinarily he would be the last person to jump into such an arrangement. He had shied away from marriage for years—and children . . .

Christian had never thought he would ever want to have kids.

But he'd been wrong.

So very wrong.

He wanted to be a father.

He wanted to be *Sissy's* father.

He wanted to be Darby's husband.

"Dammit!" he shouted to no one in particular, turning on one foot and marching in the direction of the front door.

He loved Darby, body and soul—and being a part of her life meant more to him than maintaining the status quo. Why had it taken him so long to admit such a fact to himself? Why had he hidden behind the offer of a marriage of convenience, when what he really wanted was Darby's love? Not just until he left for Thailand, but for all time.

His hands balled into fists and his jaw tightened.

He was an idiot. Only an idiot would let the situation go this far without looking into his own soul. He should have seen long ago that he had been unconsciously comparing Darby to his former wife. He'd been waiting for her to announce that she would quit her job and follow him to the ends of the earth. What he'd overlooked entirely was that Darby probably would have done just that if she wasn't chained by her own responsibilities in New York.

But he didn't care. He really didn't. Because he loved the woman enough to make his own sacrifices. He was the CEO of his own company, dammit. He could *hire* someone to take his place in Thailand. Granted, he would have to pay through the nose at this late notice, but he could afford it. He could afford anything that might mean putting his dreams within reach.

Turning, he surveyed the clinic with dawning hope, even as the little voice inside his head tried to put on the brakes.

What about the thrill of being on the job? What about those exciting locals and exotic cultures.

But even as the thought raced through his head, Christian realized that he'd grown tired of his previous life-style. He craved roots and stability. A home. A place where he belonged.

He was also a man who prided himself on learning from his mistakes—and by hell, he was going to ensure that this story ended as it should. He'd never been a man who gave things up easily, and he didn't intend to become one now. Somehow, he would convince Darby that they had to fight for what they wanted. Surely if this Compton Smythe person had any decency at all, he would realize that Sissy should never be taken away from two people who loved her so completely.

Christian was so blinded by his own emotions, that he nearly plowed over the subject of his thoughts, as Darby left the building and rushed to join him.

Not allowing her a moment to speak, he grasped her by the shoulders. "Listen to me. I don't care what Compton Smythe thinks. He doesn't have any claim at all to this baby. If he did, he would have been there when she was born. He would have known about her, cared about her. He would have comforted her, fed her and changed her diapers, dammit. He would have loved her enough to travel cross-country to see that she was happy!"

Darby's mouth opened, but before she could speak, he continued.

"We're going to fight this, do you hear? The two of us would be a much more stable influence on her life. Any judge worth his salt will have to recognize that fact. I love you. You love me. Surely a kid like Sissy deserves to live with two people who care about each other as much as we do."

Darby's eyes brimmed with unshed tears.

"You love me?"

"Of course I love you, dammit! What did you think all this was about?" he said with a vague gesture of his hand. "Do you think I'd be willing to give up a post in Thailand and take a desk job to be with anyone?"

She clutched his shirt as if to steady herself. "You want to give up your job?"

"Hell, yes. I'm in charge of Drake Enterprises, and it's time I ran it from the main office."

"But you love working on location."

"I did until I met you." He held her face up so that she couldn't mistake his earnestness. "Then I woke up to the fact that I was using my engineering status to hide from real life. To avoid the things I wanted but was sure I couldn't have."

"What kinds of things?" she whispered.

"A wife. A family. You."

"You're sure?"

"Haven't these past weeks taught you anything? I'll have you know I don't travel with just anyone. And I'm certainly not in the habit of sharing a *room* with someone I met off the street, let alone a bed."

Her eyes creased at the corners as if she were amused. "I'm glad to hear that."

"So are we going to fight this thing or not?" he demanded.

There was a beat of silence before she asked, "Am I to understand that you want to marry me right away?"

"Hell, yes."

"And that you want to complicate matters even more by accepting the responsibility of a child?"

"Of course."

"You're sure about that?"

He shook her, wondering why she was being so dense. "Don't you know how much I care about you both?"

Dropping to his knees, he took Darby's free hand. "I love you, Darby. I love you more than I ever thought I would ever love another human being. You make me laugh and tremble and fear your effect on me all at once. You make me eager for the next fifty years and beyond. You make me want to live each moment of the present to the fullest."

The tears were falling now. Openly. Sweetly.

"If you'll have me, I'll spend the rest of my life proving how much I care for you. And if you'll let me, I'll help you fight for what we both know is right. This baby should be with you, with us, as a part of *our* family."

She sobbed, bending to kiss him on the lips. "The lawyers are drawing up the papers now."

The words were so soft that Christian didn't know if he'd heard them properly.

"What?"

"Sissy's father was an anonymous sperm donor. Therefore, her legal guardianship falls to Eloise's second choice." Her smile was filled with infinite joy as she confessed, "Me. I'm to be Sissy's mother."

Christian jumped to his feet, grasping her around the waist and whirling both of the women in his life in a jubilant circle. Then, peering over her shoulder, he exclaimed to a couple of women who had appeared in the doorway. "We're going to be married, did you hear that! We're all going to be married!"

And as he hugged Darby and Sissy close, he couldn't account for the way the gray-haired woman and the too-beautiful girl seemed to know exactly what he meant.

Chapter Fourteen

Darby Simms exhaled, slowly, joyfully, then touched a hand to the wreath of orange blossoms in her hair.

Turning a slow circle, she regarded the Bridal Room of the Wedding Forum, wondering how so much could have changed in such a short amount of time. Only six weeks ago, she'd been about to marry Chauncey Fitch in this same ornate turn-of-the-century building. But today...

Today, she was about to marry her soul mate.

Her love.

Automatically she smoothed a hand over the simple antique gown that she and Christian's mother had found in a shop in upstate New York merely a week before. Although the fabric was old, the design dated, it didn't smell of mothballs. On the contrary. The dress was scented with lavender and a faint hint of cedar—as if its previous owner had experienced happy times in the gown and had cared for it dearly even after its usefulness had been spent.

Sighing happily, Darby searched the pink and gilt covered room to make sure she hadn't forgotten anything. Her gaze settled on the armoire next to the overstuffed settee and she grinned. There would be no time for television this afternoon. The Studebaker had arrived long before *she* had and was already decorated with ribbons and roses. Nor was there any reason to check ''The Gossip Exchange's'' coverage of the event since Christian had insisted on giving their reporters a front-row seat next to his parents.

Laughing, Darby scooped Sissy from the receiving blanket on the floor, fussing with the delicate lawn of the antique christening gown, which matched the eyelet found in Darby's wedding dress.

''Your daddy has a sense of humor, doesn't he?'' Darby murmured.

All in all, she couldn't think of a single worry. The legal papers to adopt Sissy had been drafted, Christian's former foreman had volunteered to take the job in Thailand, and the headquarters to Drake Enterprises had been moved to Manhattan. Even Ricardo Yvonne had surfaced from his latest conquest in time to design gowns for the mother and sisters of the groom—all the while proclaiming his gratitude to Darby for having the sense to send his latest designs into production.

The door opened and Nan Drake peeked inside.

''Ready, dear?''

''Yes,'' Darby answered eagerly.

This time, when she hesitated just outside the garden, her heart thumped with excitement and she willingly accepted the simple bouquet of roses and daisies from the elderly Forum assistant.

Nan hugged her close. "I am so happy for you both," she whispered next to Darby's ear.

Darby laughed. "No last-minute confessions?"

Nan, who was already familiar with the story of Darby's last experience at the altar, chuckled. "None other than the fact that my son loves you dearly," she said.

But Darby already knew that fact.

Nan took the baby from Darby's arms and hurried down the path, signaling to the harpist who began the wedding march. Then Darby was making her own way to the altar. This time, just as they had with Chauncey, her steps grew quicker and quicker as she approached the flower-laden bower. This time, it wasn't anger that spurred her on, but a wish to meld her life with Christian's in every way possible.

As soon as she reached his side, Christian took her hand, lacing their fingers together.

"Dearly beloved..." the pastor intoned.

His words washed over Darby in a low murmur. Somehow, she knew she would not remember everything he said, but she was sure that she would remember each wave of Christian's hair, the light in his eyes, the firm contours of his body displayed beneath the expert tailoring of his tuxedo.

When he turned to recite his vows, she watched the words as they were formed by his lips and knew that the luckiest moment of her life was when she ran from this building to find Christian at the curb. That was why she'd wanted to be married here. In the place where Fate had brought them together.

Christian lifted her hand, kissing her knuckles. Then he reached for the pillow that held the rings. It was only at that moment that Darby realized the tufted velvet held not one band but three.

Hers, a thin, engraved band.

His, a wider, more masculine circle.

And the last, a tiny, baby-size circlet.

"Oh, Christian," Darby sighed, touched beyond measure.

"We're a team, now," he murmured.

Breaking with tradition, Darby hugged him close. Yes, they were a team. Husband and wife. Mother and father and daughter.

And all because a million-dollar baby had brought them together.

AMERICAN ROMANCE®

You asked for it...You got it! More MEN!

MORE THAN MEN

We're thrilled to bring you another special edition of the popular MORE THAN MEN series.

Like those who have come before him, John Jarvis is more than tall, dark and handsome. All of those men have extraordinary powers that make them "more than men." But whether they are able to grant you three wishes, or live forever, make no mistake—their greatest, most extraordinary power is of seduction.

So make a date with John Jarvis in...

#656 RED-HOT RANCHMAN
by Victoria Pade
November 1996

HARLEQUIN®

AMERICAN ◆ ROMANCE®

It happened in an instant, but it would last a lifetime.

Suddenly

For three unlikely couples, courtship with kids is
anything but slow and easy. Meet the whole brood
as three popular American Romance authors show
you how much fun it can be in a "family affair"!

#647 CHASING BABY
by Pam McCutcheon
September 1996

#655 MARRYING NICKIE
by Vivian Leiber
November 1996

#664 ROMANCING ANNIE
by Nikki Rivers
January 1997

a Family

SAF

HARLEQUIN®
AMERICAN ◆ ROMANCE®
®

Maybe This Time...

Maybe this time...they'll get what they really wanted all those years ago. Whether it's the man who got away, a baby, or a new lease on life, these four women will get a second chance at a once-in-a-lifetime opportunity!

Four top-selling authors have come together to make you believe that in the world of American Romance anything is possible:

#642 ONE HUSBAND TOO MANY
Jacqueline Diamond
August

#646 WHEN A MAN LOVES A WOMAN
Bonnie K. Winn
September

#650 HEAVEN CAN WAIT
Emily Dalton
October

#654 THE COMEBACK MOM
Muriel Jensen
November

Look us up on-line at: http://www.romance.net

MTTG

★ Merry Christmas, Baby! ★

A romantic collection filled with the magic
of Christmas and the joy of children.

SUSAN WIGGS, Karen Young and
Bobby Hutchinson bring you Christmas wishes,
weddings and romance, in a charming
trio of stories that will warm up your
holiday season.

MERRY CHRISTMAS, BABY! also contains
Harlequin's special gift to you—a set of
FREE GIFT TAGS included in every book.

Brighten up your holiday season with
MERRY CHRISTMAS, BABY!

Available in November at
your favorite retail store.

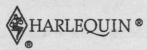

HARLEQUIN ®
®

Look us up on-line at: http://www.romance.net

MCB

REBECCA

43 LIGHT STREET

YORK

FACE TO FACE

Bestselling author Rebecca York returns to "43 Light Street"
for an original story of past secrets, deadly deceptions—and
the most intimate betrayal.

She woke in a hospital—with amnesia…and with child.
According to her rescuer, whose striking face is the last
image she remembers, she's Justine Hollingsworth. But
nothing about her life seems to fit, except for the baby
inside her and Mike Lancer's arms around her. Consumed
by forbidden passion and racked by nameless fear, she
must discover if she is Justine…or the victim of some mind
game. Her life—and her unborn child's—depends on it….

Don't miss *Face To Face*—Available in October, wherever
Harlequin books are sold.

HARLEQUIN ®

®

43FTF

1997
Reader's Engagement Book
A calendar of important dates
and anniversaries for readers to use!

Informative and entertaining—with notable
dates and trivia highlighted throughout the year.

Handy, convenient, pocketbook size to help you
keep track of your own personal important dates.

Added bonus—contains $5.00 worth of coupons
for upcoming Harlequin and Silhouette books.
This calendar more than pays for itself!

Available beginning in November at
your favorite retail outlet.

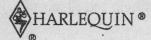

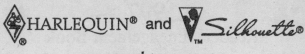
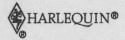